SAY IT ISN'T SO

EVA RAE THOMAS MYSTERY - BOOK 12

WILLOW ROSE

Join Willow Rose's VIP Newsletter to get exclusive updates about New Releases, Giveaways, and FREE ebooks.
Just scan this QR code with your phone and click on the link:

SCAN ME

Tired of too many emails? Text the word: "willowrose" to 31996 to sign up to Willow's VIP text List to get a text alert with news about New Releases, Giveaways, Bargains and Free books from Willow.

FOLLOW WILLOW ROSE ON BOOKBUB:

Connect with Willow online:
https://www.facebook.com/willowredrose/
https://twitter.com/madamwillowrose
http://www.goodreads.com/author/show
https://www.willow-rose.net
madamewillowrose@gmail.com

Books by the Author

HARRY HUNTER MYSTERY SERIES

- ALL THE GOOD GIRLS
- RUN GIRL RUN
- NO OTHER WAY
- NEVER WALK ALONE

MARY MILLS MYSTERY SERIES

- WHAT HURTS THE MOST
- YOU CAN RUN
- YOU CAN'T HIDE
- CAREFUL LITTLE EYES

EVA RAE THOMAS MYSTERY SERIES

- SO WE LIE
- DON'T LIE TO ME
- WHAT YOU DID
- NEVER EVER
- SAY YOU LOVE ME
- LET ME GO
- IT'S NOT OVER
- NOT DEAD YET
- TO DIE FOR
- SUCH A GOOD GIRL
- LITTLE DID SHE KNOW
- YOU BETTER RUN
- SAY IT ISN'T SO

EMMA FROST SERIES

- ITSY BITSY SPIDER
- MISS DOLLY HAD A DOLLY
- RUN, RUN AS FAST AS YOU CAN
- CROSS YOUR HEART AND HOPE TO DIE
- PEEK-A-BOO I SEE YOU
- TWEEDLEDUM AND TWEEDLEDEE
- EASY AS ONE, TWO, THREE
- THERE'S NO PLACE LIKE HOME
- SLENDERMAN
- WHERE THE WILD ROSES GROW
- WALTZING MATHILDA
- DRIP DROP DEAD
- BLACK FROST

JACK RYDER SERIES

- HIT THE ROAD JACK
- SLIP OUT THE BACK JACK
- THE HOUSE THAT JACK BUILT
- BLACK JACK
- GIRL NEXT DOOR
- HER FINAL WORD
- DON'T TELL

REBEKKA FRANCK SERIES

- ONE, TWO...HE IS COMING FOR YOU
- THREE, FOUR...BETTER LOCK YOUR DOOR
- FIVE, SIX...GRAB YOUR CRUCIFIX
- SEVEN, EIGHT...GONNA STAY UP LATE
- NINE, TEN...NEVER SLEEP AGAIN
- ELEVEN, TWELVE...DIG AND DELVE

- THIRTEEN, FOURTEEN...LITTLE BOY UNSEEN
- BETTER NOT CRY
- TEN LITTLE GIRLS
- IT ENDS HERE

MYSTERY/THRILLER/HORROR NOVELS

- SORRY CAN'T SAVE YOU
- IN ONE FELL SWOOP
- UMBRELLA MAN
- BLACKBIRD FLY
- TO HELL IN A HANDBASKET
- EDWINA

HORROR SHORT-STORIES

- MOMMY DEAREST
- THE BIRD
- BETTER WATCH OUT
- EENIE, MEENIE
- ROCK-A-BYE BABY
- NIBBLE, NIBBLE, CRUNCH
- HUMPTY DUMPTY
- CHAIN LETTER

PARANORMAL SUSPENSE/ROMANCE NOVELS

- IN COLD BLOOD
- THE SURGE
- GIRL DIVIDED

THE VAMPIRES OF SHADOW HILLS SERIES

- Flesh and Blood
- Blood and Fire
- Fire and Beauty
- Beauty and Beasts
- Beasts and Magic
- Magic and Witchcraft
- Witchcraft and War
- War and Order
- Order and Chaos
- Chaos and Courage

THE AFTERLIFE SERIES

- Beyond
- Serenity
- Endurance
- Courageous

THE WOLFBOY CHRONICLES

- A Gypsy Song
- I am WOLF

DAUGHTERS OF THE JAGUAR

- Savage
- Broken

"Say it ain't so, Joe."

Said by a reporter speaking to Shoeless Joe Jackson about Jackson's admission that he cheated in the 1919 World Series.

Prologue
SATURDAY 10:45 P.M.

Chapter 1

TEN-YEAR-OLD BECKY MCCARTHY had always dreamt of going on a cruise. Most of her school friends had been on one, and she had begged for years for her parents to take her and her sister. Now, it had finally happened. With her dad being a famous NFL-player, it wasn't because her parents didn't have the money for something like this, they could easily afford it, but her dad's career just took up so much time; there was rarely room for a family vacation. Plus, her dad didn't really like doing it much because of all the attention he usually drew to himself and all the autographs he had to sign. Usually, he never wanted to go anywhere. So, this was a big deal for all of them. Yet it was disappointing to Becky to notice that it didn't seem like they were enjoying the trip as much as she had anticipated. Her mom, Tina, had barely spoken a word all day and had been drinking a lot of colored fruity drinks at the bar by the pool upstairs. Her speech had become slurred, and her eyes glossy. Becky wasn't used to seeing that in her mom, but she often went to her friend Abriana's house, and her mom spoke like that and had that look in her eyes too.

"Mom, Mom, look at me!"

Becky yelled at the top of her lungs to get her mother's attention. Once she turned her head and looked in her daughter's direction, Becky jumped in the water, holding her nose as she curled up into a ball and made a huge splash. She twirled inside the water and came to the surface with a big smile. But as she looked toward her mother, she was gone, and the lounge chair was empty. Becky searched to see if she could find her and spotted her red one-piece swimsuit by the bar, where she was getting another of those fruity drinks with a straw.

Becky sighed, crawled up from the pool, and then sat on the edge. Her father and baby sister Nicky had gone off the ship to see Nassau and the Bahamas, where they had docked for the day. Her mom said she didn't want to go; she wanted to stay on the ship, and Becky had decided to stay with her and play in the pool. Now, she wished she had gone with her father and sister instead.

This was no fun.

Becky crossed her arms in front of her chest and pouted. She could hear her mother giggling in the bar as some guy talked to her. It bothered Becky. She shouldn't be talking to him. She was a married woman.

"Hi, B, where's Mom?"

She looked up and saw her father, then smiled. Her three-year-old sister, Nicky, was eating ice cream and had chocolate smeared around her mouth. She looked annoyingly happy. She probably had a great day while Becky was stuck with her stupid mom.

Becky looked toward the bar and noticed her dad's shoulders slump. "Oh," he simply said.

"She's been there all day while you were gone," Becky said. She looked at her younger sister, who was finishing the last bit of her ice cream and licking the melted chocolate off her fingertips. Becky felt a pang of hunger in her stomach and realized she hadn't eaten all day.

"Why is Mommy being weird?"

Her dad sighed deeply. "She's going through some stuff."

"Can I get an ice cream, Daddy?" she asked.

"Of course, honey," he said. "You go and get one while I talk to your mom. Take your sister, okay?"

Becky nodded. She grabbed her sister's hand and pulled her.

"But I want my mommy," Nicky said.

"Come on now, Nicky. Mommy had too much to drink. She can't deal with you right now," Becky said and pulled harder.

"Mommy," Nicky said with a sniffle and walked with her reluctantly. "I want my mommy."

Chapter 2

"GOOD NIGHT, sleep tight, don't let the bedbugs bite."

Becky's dad placed his finger on her nose, and she giggled.

"If they do, grab a shoe and beat them blue," she said.

That made him smile. He leaned over and kissed her forehead, then tucked the comforter around her tightly the way she preferred. Nicky was already asleep next to her in the bed they shared. She looked like a little angel with her closed eyes and both arms above her head. Becky grew sad.

"Is Mommy gonna be okay?"

Her dad looked toward the cabin's balcony, where their mom sat with a drink on the table next to her. The ship had taken off out to sea again. They were going to a private island with a waterpark the next day. Becky was really looking forward to that, and this time, she was getting off the ship no matter what. It was all she had dreamed of.

"Yeah."

He tried to smile, but Becky could sense the sadness behind it. It made her feel bad for him.

Poor Daddy.

"I'm sure she will be," he continued. "Grown-ups go through stuff from time to time. She'll get better. Don't you worry about her, okay? You get some shut-eye, so you're rested for the waterpark tomorrow. It's gonna be epic."

He kissed her again, and she smiled at the thought of the huge water slides she had seen in the pictures online that her dad had shown her. It tickled her stomach and made it harder to fall asleep as her dad left her bedside and walked out on the balcony to be with her mom.

She watched him sit beside her and try to grab her hand in his, but she pulled it away. Becky sighed, then closed her eyes again.

You gotta get some sleep. Can't be tired tomorrow.

Becky tried to think of something besides her parents and the waterslides—something boring like her science class and her teacher Miss Poletti, and it worked. She felt herself doze off, but then loud voices woke her up. She gasped and looked outside, where her mom and dad were arguing loudly.

Oh, no, not again!

Becky stared at them, worried that they would be fighting this way the next day too—on the day that was supposed to be the most perfect one of her young life. Their fighting would ruin everything.

Why did they have to fight like that?

Becky felt tears press behind her closed eyes and sniffled while trying to force herself to fall asleep. She did her best to ignore the loud voices from the other side of the sliding glass doors, but as they grew in strength, it became harder and harder for her to do so. She opened her eyes again and watched her dad grab her mom by the wrists. They were standing up now. Her dad's face was torn in anger. Becky gasped. She had never seen him like this. Her mom pulled her arms free and yelled something at him, such hatred in her eyes. It terrified Becky, and she started to cry. Her mom then pushed her dad. He pushed her back.

Please, stop. Please, just stop!

Becky's mom walked to the sliding door and opened it, then

walked inside. Her dad followed closely behind her. He was still yelling.

"That's right. You run away. That's what you always do when things get a little hard."

"The kids are sleeping, Bryan," she said, hushing him. She pointed at Becky, who closed her eyes fast, so they wouldn't realize she was awake.

She heard her dad step inside and close the door behind him. Her mom grabbed her phone and a key card for the room.

"Where do you think you're going?"

"I can't be here," she said. "I'm leaving, Bryan. I can't... I can't stand even to look at you."

"You're not going anywhere. You hear me?"

Becky cracked open her eyes just enough to peek at them. She saw her dad grab her mom by the shoulders as she went for the door. Her mom turned around and pushed his hand away.

"Stop. Tina."

Becky's mother paused and looked down. She didn't say anything for a few seconds. Then, she shook her head.

"I can't... I can't do this anymore. It's just... too hard."

"Don't leave, Tina. Please. Not like this. Can't we talk about it?"

Her dad's voice was cracking now. He was about to cry. Becky hadn't seen her dad cry many times but knew exactly what he sounded like when he did. It broke her heart.

Please, don't leave him. Please, stay, Mommy.

"What about the children?" he continued. "You can't just leave them? We're a family, remember?"

"I can't go on... I'm sorry," her mother said. "I thought I could do this, but I can't. I can't even be in the same room as you."

Then Becky heard the door open and close. She looked at her dad, who stood by the door, holding a hand to it, sobbing. He hammered his palms into it a few times while shaking his head.

Then, he opened the door and left as well. Becky finally dozed off as soon as the room went quiet and was quickly immersed in a deep dream of waterslides and ice cream.

When she woke again, someone was hovering above her, and at first, she thought this person was reaching for her necklace. But a second later, she realized this person had their hands wrapped around her neck. She gasped for air and managed to turn her head just enough to see her baby sister in the bed next to her and found her lying still, too still. Her eyes were open, and she was staring at the ceiling above. Becky waited for her to blink, but she didn't.

Part I

SATURDAY 10:45 P.M.

Chapter 1

"COME ON, SIS."

Elena Gasgarth put her hands to her sides and sighed. "I said no."

Travis threw out his arms, visibly annoyed with her. "You can help me out this one time."

She shook her head and grabbed her cart with all the cleaning supplies. She was done for the day; no more rooms to clean on her floor. She was exhausted. "You keep saying that, but it's never the last time, is it?"

"I just need some cash for the table. It won't be much. I'll be in and out fast; no one will notice. I promise."

She shook her head. "You say that every time. I risk my job doing this, so you can play Texas Hold 'Em in the casino and lose. You're so stupid. You will never win anything."

She pushed the cleaning cart and began to walk away from him. She was sick of him and his gambling. He knew she was too weak to say no to him. She simply couldn't. He would ask to get her master key card, go into rooms when people were out of their rooms, and then steal cash they left behind. It had so far been okay, and no one noticed. But it was getting too risky. One of the other cleaning ladies onboard had noticed that Travis was there a lot and commented on it. Elena just told her that he was a sucker for the casino, but she was worried that this girl was onto them.

"I won last night," Travis said, blocking her cart. "That's why I want to continue tonight. I'm on a lucky streak."

She looked at her brother. They had been through so much together since their mother killed herself when Travis was only twelve. She was the only parent they knew, so they had gone through several foster homes since then, one miserable experience after another. And as the big sister, it had always been her job to protect him. But she couldn't protect him from himself. That was the hard part.

"You're gonna get us both in a lot of trouble," she said firmly, hoping it would make him stop, yet also knowing her brother well enough to realize that it wouldn't. "I don't like it."

"Come on, Elena. You don't have to do anything. Just tell me who is out of their cabin right now and give me your keycard, then I'll do the rest."

"But you risk getting caught, and then they'll come after me. Don't you get it? I like this job. I enjoy working here."

"How? How will they ever know it had anything to do with you?" he asked. "You're the cleaning lady. Who would suspect you?"

"I have the key to each and every room here. Of course, they will. Are you stupid?" She wrinkled her forehead and gave him a stern look.

"We've done this many times before, sis. I only take the cash they leave out. They won't even notice or miss any of it. People here get so drunk they have no idea what money they have lying around. I promise you. No one has noticed yet."

"Not yet. But they will."

He shook his head. "Nonsense. Besides, I will win tonight. I can feel it. I'll share my winnings with you, okay?"

She sighed and put her hands in her pockets, feeling the keycard between her fingers—the master key card that could open any door on this floor.

He smiled charmingly, then folded his hands in front of his chest. He was so handsome, and she felt so guilty for all he had been through. The poor kid had seen too much. She had always wanted to take care of him ever since he was the one who found their mother in the bathtub at their house.

"Please?"

She rolled her eyes at him, then pulled out the card and handed it to him.

"Fine. But if you're caught, then you stole it from me. I knew nothing about it. Understood?"

He smiled widely, then grabbed the card from between her fingers.

"Understood."

He waved the card at her as he walked away. "I'll get this baby straight back to you as soon as I can, okay?"

He walked backward for a few steps while she yelled at him. "Room 873 just left. I saw them leave. But make sure you get in and out fast because they might be back soon. There was money on the side table earlier when I cleaned their room. Might still be there."

"You got it, sis. In and out fast. That's my middle name."

She scoffed and shook her head. Then, she grabbed the cart and pushed it down the hallway, saying a silent prayer for her brother not to get caught.

Chapter 2

TRAVIS SLID the card through the reader, then looked over both shoulders before pushing the door open to room 873. He let it slide shut behind him, closing it completely. He held his breath for a second while scanning the room to make sure there really was no one there. If there were, if somehow it was a mistake and they had come back, he would pretend to be an electrician and tell them that he had been called to their room because there was something wrong with the AC, then act like it was the wrong room and leave. It had happened once before, and they had bought the lie with no questioning.

But it had left him worried it might happen again every time he entered a room. He started to breathe properly again when seeing no one there.

You're good. They're gone. Do your thing, then get out of there.

"My winning hand awaits," he mumbled to himself with a grin. He had been so close to the big win the night before; he could still taste the sweet victory. It was going to come tonight; he knew it would. He could feel it in his bones.

And then, he would never have to steal petty cash again.

He walked toward the bed by the window, then looked at the small table next to it.

Bingo.

His sister had been right; there was a pile of bills right there. He grabbed them and flipped through them. Mostly twenties, but as he came further down the stack, there were a couple of hundreds tucked in there too.

He slid the hundreds into his pocket, then put the twenties back on the table. This way, they wouldn't notice until way later, and by then, they'd just assume that they might have spent them somewhere. They might even fight about it, blaming each other for spending too much money.

Travis smiled at the thought while he scanned the room to see if these people had carelessly left more cash out somewhere. He even went to the drawers by the mirror on the side wall of the room and pulled them out one after the other. Carefully, he went through their contents without making a mess and risking them getting suspicious. When he pulled open the second drawer, he smiled widely.

A wallet. Someone had left a red leather wallet inside it. He opened it, pulled out two hundred-dollar bills, and put them in his pocket; then, he closed the drawer. He often liked to imagine their faces when realizing the money was gone. While onboard, people usually didn't need cash since food was included, and if they got the drink package, they could drink as much alcohol, tea, coffee, or sodas as they wished from any of the bars or restaurants onboard. Most people did that, so they never needed their wallets—not until the ship docked in the Bahamas and people went onshore to buy silly souvenirs. By then, they might realize that the money was gone, but they'd often think they got robbed by some local pickpocket. They would never guess it actually happened onboard.

Travis counted the bills he had found and was satisfied when he realized there was five hundred dollars there. It would be enough for a good night of gambling, and hopefully, he'd win big this time—like he almost did the night before.

I was so close.

He turned around, then got ready to leave the room, scanning it to make sure everything looked the same as when he entered it. He then walked toward the door, but as he passed the toilet to his right side, something made him stop. The door was left ajar.

Travis's heart beat faster as he gently pushed the door open to the toilet and peeked inside.

What he saw on the other side made him want to scream so badly that he had to bite his finger until it started to bleed in order not to do so.

Chapter 3

AS THE PLANE hit more turbulence, I closed my eyes and tried to picture my children. I lined them up in my mind, with my oldest, Ollie, first, then Christine, Alex, and finally Angel, my baby Angel. As the plane bumped forward, I was lifted out of my seat. I let out a small shriek, then turned to look at Isabella Horne, the FBI director, who had picked me up at home that same morning, telling me we needed to get on a plane asap. She said she would brief me while in the air, and that's what she was trying to do, but I was barely listening. Flying on small planes wasn't my thing. I had never liked heights, and this was just awful for me.

"Are you listening, Eva Rae?" she asked.

I opened my eyes and looked at her. "Not really. How can you focus when we're about to die?"

Isabella laughed. "You think this is bad? You should try flying locally in Nicaragua. That's scary."

"When did you ever do that?" I asked, feeling my croissant from this morning as it made its reentry, threatening to leave my body. I felt so nauseated.

"You don't want to know," she said.

"No, probably not."

The plane calmed down slightly, and I eased up. I tried not to look out the window but focused on the pilot in front of us. He didn't seem to be in any distress, so that was a good sign.

"You say no one has seen anything of the two children since yesterday?" I asked, letting her know that I had been listening after all.

"Exactly. Nicky, three years old, and Becky, ten years old, both disappeared from their room sometime after nine o'clock. Crew members say the family left the restaurant at seven fifteen when the dad signed the bill. The dad reported them missing at eleven forty-five to the Chief Security Officer onboard. The dad last saw them and the mother at a little after nine o'clock when he left the room."

"How do we know they're not just sleeping somewhere on the ship? That they left their room and went somewhere else to sleep? It's a big ship."

"One of the biggest in the world. It can hold up to six thousand passengers and is nineteen stories tall. It left Nassau in the Bahamas yesterday afternoon at five, then docked at the cruise line's private island right after midnight, but due to the missing children and mother, no one has been allowed to leave the ship."

I looked at my watch. It was almost noon. "I bet that's popular."

"Yeah, well, we have more important issues. The ship's people have searched the restaurants, stores, and every corner of the ship, yet no sign of the children or their mother. That's why they got nervous—they can't let anyone off the ship until they are found. They called for help, and since it has to do with missing children…."

"The FBI is the answer," I said. "The ship is in Bahamian waters; are we allowed to?"

"The Crimes and Criminal Procedure Code, Title 18 of the U.S.C., states that The Bureau is authorized to investigate the kidnapping of any U.S. national on any ship that docks or departs from any port in the United States," she said. "Since this one departed from Cape Canaveral, we're good to go."

"What do the parents say?"

"They haven't been able to locate the mother yet, but the father is out of his mind with worry."

"Naturally. But the mother is gone too?" I asked while grabbing the armrests as the plane started to bump again. Gosh, I hated flying.

"Yes, the dad says he has no idea where she might be either. Apparently, they fought last night, and she left."

I looked at her. "Is it possible that the mom might have taken the kids?"

She shrugged. "The dad seems to think so. But where could she go? They are in the middle of the Atlantic Ocean."

"That's a darn good question," I said, seeing the small island approaching in the distance as we began our descent into the tropical paradise that was going to be like hell on earth for me over the coming hours.

Chapter 4

THEN:

"Mom, Dad, I want you to meet my girlfriend."

Bryan McCarthy made room for Tina to come closer. She smiled insecurely and shook hands with his parents. They were meeting at an Italian restaurant in downtown Sheboygan, Wisconsin. It was a place Bryan was certain would feel comfortable for Tina. After all, meeting your boyfriend's parents for the first time was a lot. He knew she loved the food there, and they had been there often, so hopefully, she would be okay.

They all sat down and ordered. It was quiet around the table for a while, making Bryan nervous.

"How about this weather we're having, huh?" his mother asked in an attempt to break the awkward silence.

"It's been nice to be able to sit outside at this time of year," his dad added. "It's been a very good summer."

"They say it's the global warming," his mother continued. "I, for one, am not complaining, though."

She ended with a light chuckle, and Bryan looked at Tina. He worried she might be put off by their comments. His parents didn't really believe in global warming and thought it was nonsense. Now, he worried Tina might think badly about them because of it. He wanted them to like one another.

To his luck, she chose to ignore it and didn't say anything. The food came, and they began to eat. Tina was fiddling with her wine glass and looking at him shyly. Gosh, how he loved her and those big blue eyes.

"Tina, what do you do?" his dad asked while putting down his wine glass.

"Right now, I'm still in school, but I'm planning on being a stay-at-home mom as soon as we're married and the children come along."

Bryan's mom almost choked on the wine in her mouth. Tina clasped her mouth. "Oh, no, did I say too much?"

"You're…you're…?" his mom stared at him, then at her.

Tina lifted her hand so they could see the ring.

"I proposed two days ago," he said. "After a game. We won."

"Of course you did, son," his dad said, tapping his shoulder. "And congratulations to you both."

"It would have been great to meet her first," his mom mumbled, but the dad put a hand on her arm to make her stop. She looked up at him. "But what if they're rushing into things?"

"Bryan is a busy man with a great career. They're telling us now, and we're meeting her now. We're very happy for you, son," he said. He smiled at Tina, then raised his glass. "To the couple."

They all clinked glasses while Bryan felt like he was suffocating. He wanted to tell them earlier, but to be honest, he was scared of their reaction in case they thought he was rushing into things. He was still very young and about to be drafted into the NFL. His agent said it was very close now. He couldn't have too many distractions. Not now.

He felt Tina's hand in his. "I will support your son's career all the way," she said. "I believe he can be one of the greatest, and with the right woman behind him, he will achieve all his goals. I believe a woman's place is with her man, supporting him, taking care of the children."

She winked at him, and he relaxed his shoulders. Then he kissed her, closing his eyes. His friends had asked him if he had any doubts before proposing to Tina, and of course, he had. No one was perfect. But all the doubts he had vanished completely in this precious moment as their lips met.

"I think you found yourself a good one there, son," his dad said and put his hand on his shoulder. "You have fought too hard and come too far to let someone steal the spotlight, and this one will let you be the star that you are. That is rare these days. Everyone and her mother wants to have a career. And when you do find someone like that, you better put a ring on her finger before someone else does. Well done, son. Well done."

Chapter 5

THE LANDING on the island was the worst, and for a few minutes, I was certain this was the end of the line for me. We hopped and bumped, and I was tossed around inside the small cabin until we finally set the wheels on solid ground, and I dared to open my eyes again.

The view was spectacular—almost a cliché—azure-blue—close to green—ocean, palm trees, and white sandy beaches as far as I could see. It was gorgeous. It was the cruise line's private island that they docked at with their passengers for the day. It even had a waterpark with colorful slides towering in the distance. There was no airport on the island, but we landed on a small strip of grass that was used to bring in planes with supplies.

I can't tell you how good it felt to walk out of that plane and feel the grass beneath my shoes. A golf cart came to pick us up and rushed us through the small island. We passed many bars, restaurants, and small souvenir stands selling trinkets and clothes on our way.

"It docked here late last night," Isabella said, pointing at the ship towering in the distance. It was enormous. I had seen it many times before in the distance when it left Cape Canaveral, and several times a week, it would pass Cocoa Beach out in the ocean, but I had never seen it up close.

"And the passengers have been staying there since then?" I asked and looked at my watch. I knew they only had one day here, so I guessed they were all pretty angry that they couldn't leave the ship.

"Yup. The ship's security team and the rest of the personnel have been combing through the ship since they were reported missing—with no results."

"Could they have fallen overboard?" I asked.

She shrugged. "All three of them? It would be strange."

"Have we had the coast guard out here to search the waters?" I asked.

"The cruise ship used boats and lights in the waters until the coast guard arrived and took over. They have been searching the ocean with boats and helicopters for hours around the area where the ship was when the children were reported missing, with no luck. It's Bahamian waters, and we have to rely on the Bahamian police and coast guard, which…."

"Isn't the most efficient in the world. I get it. Why didn't the ship turn around?"

"It is believed that the children are hiding somewhere. None of the surveillance cameras show anyone falling overboard. I'm still holding onto the hope that they're somewhere on the ship. Otherwise, it will be very hard to find them. This is a big ocean."

I stared at the ship, then at the Atlantic Ocean behind it as we neared the entrance, and the golf cart stopped. It looked like a floating skyscraper.

"I won't be able to stay for long," Isabella said as we walked up the gangway and showed our badges to the security waiting for us. "I am needed on another case back west, so I'll just make sure you're settled in properly and then leave you in charge of the investigation. Toby Clover here will help you—he and his crew. He's the chief security officer. Like all major cruise lines, they have sophisticated security departments run by former federal, state, and military law enforcement officials. They also have medical staff onboard: one trained doctor and two nurses. They're located at the infirmary below deck."

I nodded and followed Toby inside the ship. "I'm gonna start with the surveillance cameras. We're gonna need to go through all of them from last night. And not just the ones covering the area outside. I want the inside ones too. Especially those closest to the room they're in."

Isabella's phone rang, and she picked it up while we rushed through the ship and up through what looked like the mall area of a small town, with shops, bars, and restaurants on all sides. People were hanging out, eating food, and sipping their big colorful cups of alcoholic beverages. It had me worried. A lot of angry people were about to get very drunk, and that wasn't going to end well.

"All right," she said when she hung up. "I'm afraid I'm going to have to leave now. Will you be okay? If you need anything, let me know. And Eva Rae?"

"Yes, I know. Find the kids alive. I'll do my best."

She placed a hand on my shoulder.

"I know you will. That's why I brought you here."

Chapter 6

HIS HANDS FELT CLAMMY, and his shirt was sticking to his chest. It wasn't that it was particularly hot inside his stateroom cabin, but he was getting exceedingly nervous as the hours moved on.

Travis hadn't talked to his sister since the night before; he had stayed in his room while listening to the emergency broadcast being announced. They weren't saying "Mr. Mob" or "Oscar," which were usually the codes for *man overboard*, which his sister had taught him. That made him think they still believed the children were on the ship.

Travis bit his fingernails, not knowing how to deal with this. There was a search going on for those two little children.

What am I going to do?

Travis wiped the sweat from his forehead with a towel, then continued staring at the door to his room like he expected it to burst open suddenly and the police to come storming in.

He could barely breathe.

Travis looked at his watch and realized it was late. He hadn't left his room all day, and now the hunger was getting to him. He needed food and water. If he was perfectly honest, he could really use a drink right about now, too—or maybe a couple.

He grabbed his keycard, then left the room, looking over his shoulders as he walked out. As he took the elevator upstairs toward the restaurants, his heart was hammering in his chest.

Just do it quickly. Pretend like everything is normal. Go in, ask for some food to bring to your room, then leave. Go back into hiding.

He spotted the small Irish pub as soon as he got out of the elevator. It was the closest restaurant. He walked inside, tried to smile, then asked the young girl behind the counter for a grilled ham sandwich and maybe a beer.

"To go, please."

"Of course," she said with a gentle smile, and he felt himself relax. She didn't seem suspicious of him.

"And a couple of bottled waters, too," he added.

"You got it."

She disappeared into the back for what felt like forever. Meanwhile, he stared into the corridor where people were walking by, pushing strollers, drinking their drinks, and chatting. Some looked bored; others seemed to be making the best of their time on the ship since they weren't allowed to leave.

At the center of the corridor, the crew had set up a show, where some crew members were dancing on a small glass bridge crossing the mall area of the ship, wearing eighties clothes, blasting out Madonna. They were probably trying to boost morale. It didn't seem to be working; most people just passed it, barely looking. Only a few children had stopped to watch. Travis shook his head; he knew all three crew members up there, wearing tutu skirts and pink legwarmers. He also knew how much they hated doing this.

"Why would they be dancing when children are missing?" a lady said as she entered the restaurant. Her husband shook his head, and they sat down. Travis thought about those two poor girls again, then felt how his hands began to shake. The bartender served him his beer.

"Here you go, buddy."

"Thanks," he said and grabbed it. He drank like his life depended on it, his hands clammier than ever. The dance show continued to the tunes of more Madonna, and the dancing crew members swung their arms and did their little routine while most people just shook their heads.

"I heard the FBI just got here," the woman from earlier said. She was trying to whisper but not really doing a very good job. "Some female agent. Gotta be serious if the FBI is here, right?"

"You're right about that," the husband answered.

"And I heard the mom was missing too. What do you make of that, huh?" she asked, sounding like she knew all the answers.

"I really can't say...," the husband said, sounding very uninterested in the entire conversation.

She leaned forward but still didn't really lower her voice. "I bet the husband threw them all overboard."

"How could you say something like that?" her husband said, then ordered his fish and chips.

She shrugged secretively. "Call it a hunch. It's been known to happen."

"That doesn't mean it is what happened in this case." He sounded slightly annoyed now.

"He's a famous NFL player, you know," she said, shaking her head. "I never liked him much."

"Maybe we shouldn't jump to concl...."

She continued unabated. "Or maybe the mother wanted to commit suicide and took the children with her. Had them all jump."

The husband sighed. "Or maybe they're here somewhere and fell asleep in a place where no one has been looking. Maybe they're hiding and don't want to be found."

"I don't believe that for a minute. Something is fishy about this story. One thing is for sure," she said, pointing her finger at him. "I bet you we'll never see those kids again. It's too late. They're in the ocean somewhere, and everyone knows you can't survive out there very long, even if the water is warm here. And we will never get to experience the island. I just hope they'll let us get off this darn ship soon."

"It hasn't been that long," her husband said while the server brought them their drinks.

The woman tasted her cosmopolitan, then wrinkled her nose and signaled for the server to return.

"I'm gonna need more alcohol in this if I am to make it through this day. Can you do that for me?"

The server nodded politely, then grabbed her drink and left. Travis was handed a box with his food from the smiling girl, then left. He asked for another beer before he rushed back to the elevator and took it to his floor. He hurried down the hallway and slid the key card to open his door, then walked inside, breathing heavily, closing his eyes in relief.

No one suspected him of anything.

As he set the food down on the table, the small feet sticking out from beneath the covers began to move.

Chapter 7

"CAPTAIN, I want you to meet FBI agent Eva Rae Thomas. Agent Thomas, this is Captain Larsen."

The uniformed man in front of me stepped forward and reached out his hand. I felt myself blush just from looking at him; he was so handsome. He kind of reminded me of Thor, or really the actor playing him, Chris Hemsworth. He was probably in his late forties but looked way younger.

"Larsen," I said. "That sounds Scandinavian?"

He nodded. "Norwegian, born and raised in Bergen. I've sailed my entire life. We are very pleased to have you here, Agent Thomas."

He had a heavy accent to his English that was absolutely adorable and made me smile.

"Well, I wish the circumstances would have been different," I said and let go of his firm handshake.

"You and me both."

"Tell me, Captain...."

"Call me Anders, please," he said. "Where I come from, we don't like being too formal."

I looked up at him and met his blue eyes. He seriously looked like he had stepped out of a movie. "Okay, Anders... am I saying it right?"

He smiled. "Close enough."

"All right... Anders... you have so far been in charge of this search mission. Can you fill me in, please? No detail is too small."

"Well, to be honest, I don't know a lot. But I do know that I was on the bridge at eleven twenty-two when I was alerted that two children had gone missing. I was told that the father was the one who reported it to our chief security officer, and they informed me, as is the procedure. I started a search mission, but we haven't found them —at least not yet. I have not let anyone leave the ship in case the children were taken against their will. Someone might try to get away with them. Even though it is a private island, there are still ways to get away. The people working the souvenir shops all live on other islands and come here by boat every morning and leave late at night. Someone might pay a good amount of money to smuggle out two children, and someone might succumb to the temptation."

"I'm glad you did that," I said. "Makes my job a little easier."

He smiled politely and nodded. "I just want those kids and their mother to be found."

"Do you have children?" I asked.

"Yes, two boys at home," he said. "The apple of my eye. Both of them."

"I thought so."

I paused and thought about my own children for a brief moment. They were with their grandmother while I was gone, and I could only pray that she was able to take care of all of them. My ex Matt, and the father of my youngest, was out of town at a police convention, so he couldn't take the baby. I knew my mom could deal with the three older ones just fine, but the youngest tore on her strength. She was a lot of work. I had to admit to that. But she was also super adorable and could get away with anything.

"Has security gone through the surveillance cameras?" I asked.

"We looked through all the outside ones," the captain said. "To see if they had fallen overboard or maybe even jumped. It is standard procedure when a person goes missing on a cruise ship."

"And you didn't see anything, I was told?"

He shook his head. "Luckily, no. And there have been no witnesses. Usually, in these cases, and it does happen from time to time that a passenger or crew member jumps, there's at least one witness who saw what happened. It usually involves a lot of alcohol beforehand, which is why we have the cameras in place. It's required of us. Of course, we can't see if someone falls from a room balcony."

I nodded. It was good news that no one had seen them jump or fall. That meant they could still be somewhere on the ship. I wanted to hold onto that because it gave me hope—hope that I might find them alive.

"I'm going to need your men to start going through the footage from inside the ship," I said. "It's gonna be a big job, but I need them to look for the mom and the children. I assume you have been provided with pictures of all three of them by the dad?"

"Yes, and I will make sure they get on it asap. Anything else you want me to do?"

"I need to talk to the dad. Please."

Chapter 8

THEN:

"Congratulations, you two."

Tina looked briefly at Bryan, then smiled.

"Thank you," she said as the woman who had congratulated them kissed her cheek, then moved on.

Bryan couldn't stop staring at her. She was beyond gorgeous in that big white dress. To be honest, he had never seen any woman so beautiful. And as of half an hour ago, she became his when they said the famous "I do" to one another, and the pastor declared them husband and wife.

Any prettier words didn't exist.

She was his wife. He was her husband.

Finally.

Bryan had been drafted to the NFL for the Green Bay Packers, and all his teammates were at the reception, most of them goofing around and making fun of him for being a kept man now.

The old ball and chain.

He didn't mind. As a matter of fact, he was excited about this new chapter in his life—more than excited. He was thrilled and so, so very happy. He was happier than any of them, even if they did tease him and let him know that he would miss out on all the female fans they always hooked up with after games.

That chapter was over for him now—no more other women. There was just this one for him.

His wife.

"Should we cut the cake?" she asked, her eyes sparkling.

"Sure," he said, and they walked to the tower of a wedding cake she had ordered from one of the most expensive bakeries in Green Bay, where they lived now. It was almost nine feet tall and nearly reached the stucco ceiling at the beautiful old buildings of Hotel Northland, where the wedding reception was being held. Outside the windows, paparazzi were waiting for them to walk back out once it was over. They had taken a ton of pictures of all the guests as they walked in earlier. There was nothing like a wedding to get them all riled up.

That was what Bryan hated the most about the job as an NFL player. But it came with the territory. He was still pretty new to the whole thing, so they probably weren't there for him. But some of his teammates had been in the game for a long time and were regular celebrities. The paparazzi loved them.

Tina grabbed the knife, then smiled at Bryan while holding it. She placed it on the cake, then waited for him to put his hand on it too. The knife slid through the thick frosting, and people took photos. Tina smiled at the cameras, and Bryan did his best to match her. They cut a big piece, then got it on the plate, and Bryan fed her the first bite as tradition directed it.

Everyone clapped.

Tina lifted her arms in the air like she had won something, then laughed with her mouth full.

It was so endearing that Bryan couldn't stop looking at her, smiling secretively.

Then, they kissed—a long and passionate kiss that made the crowd cheer even louder and made Bryan smile even wider.

Nothing could go wrong at this moment. Everything was perfect.

Chapter 9

HE WAS SITTING on a chair inside the captain's quarters behind the bridge, holding his face between his hands when I entered. It was the most luxurious cabin with stunning views from all sides, and also where the captain slept when he wasn't working. Captain Larsen closed the door behind us. Bryan McCarthy was a big man; I could tell even though he was sitting down. He looked up, and our eyes met. He rose to his feet, his eyes torn with trouble.

"This is Agent Thomas from the FBI," the captain said.

"Agent Thomas, I'm so glad you're here," he said and walked toward me, reaching out his hand.

I shook it.

"Bryan McCarthy," he said. When I didn't react, he added. "From the Packers."

I shook my head. I knew he was some NFL player since Isabella had told me, but his name didn't ring a bell for me.

"I don't watch sports, sorry."

I placed my purse on the ground and grabbed a chair. Then I pointed at the one where he had been sitting. "Please, sit down."

We sat just as someone knocked on the door. The captain opened it.

"We have a situation," I heard a voice say from behind it.

The captain looked at me, his blue eyes concerned.

"It's fine," I said. "Go ahead."

Captain Larsen left, and the door slammed shut behind him. I started the recording and introduced who was present and the date and time, then I looked at him.

"Mr. McCarthy. Please, tell me what happened. When did you see your children last?"

He leaned forward, his broad shoulders bulging underneath his white T-shirt. He shook his head and touched his chin briefly.

"I… I don't really know where to begin. I can't believe this is happening. I mean… how… how is this even…? She took them, you know? I know she did. I just know it."

He got agitated and gesticulated wildly.

"You're talking about your wife?"

"Yes."

"Okay, let's get back to last night. Just tell me in any order you like."

He threw out his hands. "We had a fight, okay? That's why she did it."

"You and your wife?" I asked, writing it down.

"Yes. Tina and I had a fight."

"When did this fight begin?"

"It started on the first day of our vacation. Why is that relevant?"

"And that was Friday, right?"

"We came onboard Friday late afternoon and left Cape Canaveral."

"And that's when you began to argue."

"Well, it started in the car on our way to the airport, actually. Friday morning, when we were going to fly to Orlando."

"What was the fight about?" I asked.

He looked puzzled. "Is that relevant?"

"I won't know until I get more details. I know this can seem very private, but it could be important."

He blew out air, then leaned back. He seemed tired, but I guess I couldn't blame him. He hadn't slept at all.

"It was nothing. Can't you just write down on your notepad that she took them? She took my children, and I'm worried about what she did to them."

"Let's get back to last night. You were fighting, you say? Then what happened?" I asked.

"She left around nine o'clock. The kids had fallen asleep, and she began to argue again. She loves to nitpick and discuss things until you want to scream, and I was sick of it. I just wanted to enjoy my vacation, sit on my balcony and look out over the ocean, you know?"

"She left? Then what happened?"

"I left a little later."

"You went after her?"

"I did. I was afraid of what she might do. She hasn't been right for some time, and I feared she might jump."

"You thought she might kill herself?" I asked, surprised at this news. No one had mentioned this before.

He nodded. "She was unstable—drunk. She had been drinking all day on the ship. She wasn't in a good place."

"And where were the kids at this time?"

"They were sleeping in our cabin. I thought they were fine since we were the only ones with a key to the room. Becky is ten years old and could easily take care of the little one should they both wake up. Besides, it was important for me to find Tina before she did something stupid."

I nodded to ensure he knew I wasn't accusing him of being a bad dad. I understood his choice, even though I wasn't sure I would have done the same.

"What happened next?" I asked.

"I couldn't find her anywhere. I searched everywhere on the outside of the ship. It was very windy, and no one was out there. I didn't find her either. So, I walked back to the cabin."

"And what time was this?"

"Around eleven o'clock."

"You'd been walking around for about two hours searching for her?" I asked.

"Yes. That sounds about right."

"Okay, then what?"

"I... I returned and used my keycard to get back in, and then...." He clasped his mouth and took a break before continuing. "And then... they were gone. Their bed was empty."

"That must have been pretty scary?"

He swallowed and could barely look at me. His eyes were tearing up, and I could tell he was embarrassed that he couldn't keep them at bay. I guessed that he didn't often cry in his line of work.

"It was terrifying. I couldn't believe it. I called their names and looked in the bathroom, but I knew they weren't there. I knew they were gone, that she... that she had taken them."

"This was your conclusion right away when realizing they were gone? That your wife had taken them?"

"I just knew it in my heart."

I nodded in empathy. "And then what did you do?"

"I ran into the hallway and found a crew member who could take me to security, where I reported it."

"You didn't go looking for her and the kids first?" I asked. "They could have gone to grab a bite to eat?"

He shook his head. "I just knew that she had done something awful. I *knew* it."

Chapter 10

THE KNOCK on his door sounded like pounding to Travis—like someone was trying to break down the door. He got scared when it started, and sweat sprang again from his forehead.

Was it the police?

"Travis! Open up!"

Travis breathed again. It was his sister's voice.

"Travis, I know you're in there; open up, please, or I'll use my key."

Travis jumped to his feet and hurried to the door. He took a deep breath before opening it and sliding into the hallway where Elena stood. He pulled the door shut behind him.

"What's up, sis?"

"*What's up, sis?* Is that all you have to say?" she asked, placing her hands on her hips in her maid's uniform.

"I… guess so? Is there something I missed?" he asked, forcing a smile.

She scrutinized him. "Why are you being weird?"

"I'm not. I swear. I was just… taking a nap."

She looked like she had figured something out. She pointed her finger at him. "You got a girl in there, don't you?"

He felt like the blood left his face. "A girl? No, no. No girls."

She smiled. "Yes, you do. You hooked up with someone, and she's still in there. Why do you feel embarrassed about that, Travis? I know how you are. You could have told me, and I would have left right away. At least you're making something out of a bad situation. Meanwhile, I am running around out here, and people are constantly asking me what is going on and when they can leave the ship. Like I would know, right? I clean rooms, that's all."

"Oh, I bet that's annoying," he answered without even listening. His heart was hammering in his chest, and he was feeling dizzy now.

"People are getting pissed; I'm telling you. A lot of people are getting drunk, and it's only very early afternoon. It's not good. They're angry. It's like a pressure cooker right now, waiting to blow. Two men got into a fight at the bakery, and the security officers had to detain them and call the captain. It's only a matter of time before they turn their anger on the crew. I really hope they find those missing kids soon—before this whole place blows up."

"Wow, that sounds awful," he said.

"I actually came here to ask if you wanted to grab some food. I'm on my break now, but I guess you're busy, huh?"

He nodded, sweat springing from his upper lip. He wiped it away with the back of his hand, then smiled awkwardly.

Elena narrowed her eyes. "I still say you're acting strange. What's going on with you? Something is up."

He stared at her with his eyes wide, heart knocking against his ribcage. "S-something is u-up? What do you mean?"

"Oh, I know," she said with a small gasp.

"You do?"

His voice went up.

"Oh, my God, Travis. Is she someone I know? She is, isn't she? You promised me you wouldn't sleep with any of my colleagues again. Travis! It's so embarrassing for me when you ghost them, and they keep coming to me for advice. How I hate you."

Travis smiled. He felt awful, but this was the best for right now. He threw out his arms. "What can I say? I'm a pig. Is that illegal?"

Elena looked at him, then growled, annoyed. She turned around and left.

He glared after her as she walked away, then mumbled under his breath. "I'm sorry, sis. It's for your own good. Please, forgive me."

Chapter 11

"THIS IS WHERE THEY WERE SLEEPING."

Bryan pointed at the bed closest to the door. There were two queen-sized beds in the cabin, a sitting area with a couch, and a coffee table. His cabin was a suite with a small office and a desk too. It was the biggest cabin I had seen and almost as big as the captain's.

"The last time I saw them."

Bryan stared at the bed, his shoulders slumped.

"They looked so cute, so innocent... I never... I should never have left them. I should have just stayed... I...."

He lifted his gaze and looked at me, turning his head toward me.

"I could have stopped her. Had I been here, she would never have been able to...," he paused and lowered his eyes. "I failed them."

"There's still hope," I said, "that we may find them."

He rubbed his eyes and shook his head while I walked around the suite. I stared at the balcony, then at the sliding door leading to it outside. I walked closer, then looked at it, focusing on the area around the handle.

"Do you see anything?" he asked.

I stared at it for a little while longer, then shook my head. "I thought I did, but I was wrong."

I glared at the sparkling ocean on the other side of the glass. Bryan came closer.

"Do you think she might have thrown them overboard and then jumped?" he asked, terror in his voice. "There are no surveillance cameras on the private balconies."

I shook my head. "I don't know. I really hope not."

"What kind of a mother would do such a thing?" he asked, sobbing.

"Let's not get carried away here," I said. "I still have hope that they're onboard somewhere."

He nodded. "You're right. There might still be hope."

I turned around, pushing back the images in my mind of the poor kids out in the ocean. I couldn't think like that. I had to focus.

I walked back to the bed where they had been sleeping. The covers were pulled to the side, and the white sheet was messed up and had slipped off the edges at the left side of the bed and was almost pulled off the sides. The pillows were messed up; one had fallen to the floor.

"The flat sheet is missing," I said.

"What's that?"

I pointed at the bed. "The duvet cover is here, but the flat sheet isn't."

"Hm," he said. "That's strange. Maybe we never had one?"

I looked at him for a few seconds, then returned to stare at the empty bed.

A teddy bear was on the right side of the bed by the feet, half hidden under the covers. I leaned forward and looked at it.

"That is Nicky's," he said. "My little girl. She's only three years old. She can't sleep without it."

"I know how that goes," I said and turned around. "My daughter has a dinosaur that she absolutely can't live without, and I am definitely not allowed to wash it, even if it is a health hazard."

I looked toward the bathroom, then walked to the door and pushed it open. It was pretty big for a cruise ship bathroom. There were toiletries left out next to the sink and a small bag with make-up that I assumed belonged to the mother. There were four tooth-brushes and two different kinds of toothpaste, one for the adults and one for the children. Nothing seemed out of order.

I walked back into the room, then looked at Bryan. "Does anything seem out of the ordinary to you?"

He shook his head. "Except for the fact that my family is missing? No. It all looks like it did when I left."

"And there's no sign of a break-in, so…."

"Actually, wait a minute," he said.

"Yes?"

He walked to the side table and looked at a pile of money. "My money is missing."

"Excuse me?"

He flipped through the pile. "Not all of it, but all the one-hundred-dollar bills. I know there were some in there."

He turned to stare at me, his eyes puzzled.

"Wait a second," he added, then walked to the drawers underneath the mirrors. He pulled one out and then grabbed a red wallet from inside it. He opened it, then looked at me.

"My wife's money is gone too!" He showed me the empty wallet. "Look!"

"But…?"

He threw out his arms in agitation. "We've been robbed! I can't believe it!"

Chapter 12

THEN:

He grabbed another glass of champagne as the waitress walked by with them on her tray, serving the guests. Bryan sipped the tall drink and glanced at Tina, who was surrounded by her pink bridesmaids. They were giggling and talking with big smiles on their faces. Tina grabbed a salmon quiche appetizer as the waiter walked past her, then glanced toward Bryan. As their eyes met, they both smiled. Bryan felt like he hadn't stopped smiling since he saw her walk down the aisle in that dress. His cheeks were hurting, but that didn't matter.

The DJ was playing Michael Jackson's *I Just Can't Stop Loving You*, and Bryan mimicked the words to her. That made her laugh and throw her head back. Then he signaled for her to come to him. He could tell she told her friends, "Excuse me for a minute," and then left them. She approached him, and they took each other's hands.

"I think it's time for our dance soon," she whispered.

"I've been looking forward to it," he said.

"Really? I didn't think you liked to dance?"

"Well, I've been taking lessons."

She looked at him, surprised. "You have? Oh, my God, that's the sweetest thing ever. Thank you."

She kissed him, and he closed his eyes while taking in the smell of her. Everything about this girl was just so perfect.

How was that even possible?

How did he get to be this lucky?

He sighed deeply as he opened his eyes and saw a woman standing behind her. "Oh, my Auntie Emma." He took Tina's hand in his and turned her around. "Tina, I want you to meet my dear Aunt Emma. You remember I told you about her? She took care of my brother and me when my mom was sick for three years, battling cancer."

"Luckily, she beat it," Aunt Emma said and winked. "So she can be here today and experience this wonderful day, seeing her son getting married. What could be better?" She grabbed Bryan's face between her hands, then kissed his cheeks.

"How have you been, my boy? It's been too long. You look handsome, but boy have you grown; look at those muscles."

"Aunt Emma moved to Florida ten years ago, and I have barely seen her since," he said. "You look great, too, though. Doesn't she look great, Tina?"

Tina smiled and pulled the small woman into a deep hug. "Aunt Emma, I have heard a lot about you. I'm so glad to have finally met you."

"Oh, likewise, my dear," Aunt Emma said. "Aren't you a lively one? You are beautiful, my dear. That white dress fits you like a glove, slim as you are. But I always knew my boy would find someone as gorgeous as you. He has good taste. He gets it from me, but don't tell his mom that."

They laughed as Auntie Emma elbowed Tina and winked at her.

"My lips are sealed," she said. "Say, is your husband with you today?"

Bryan's smile froze for the first time that day. He exhaled. Auntie Emma looked distressed.

"What?" Tina asked, confused. "Did I say something wrong?"

Auntie Emma shook her head and placed her hand on top of Tina's. "No, my dear. You couldn't have known. My late husband died in the nine-eleven attacks. He was a firefighter and ran into the north tower just before it collapsed."

Auntie Emma looked down, then up at Tina. Tina pulled her hand away and clasped her mouth.

"Oh, Lord, I am so sorry."

Auntie Emma gave Bryan a look.

"Well, Bryan should have told you, but no one in the family likes to talk about it. It still hurts, you know. Peter was a very loved man and the best husband I could imagine—maybe except for your Bryan here. He will make an excellent one as well."

"I'm so sorry," Tina said again, placing a hand on the woman's shoulder. "I really didn't know…. To think that you lost your husband in that awful government coverup is just appalling."

Aunt Emma's eyes grew serious, and soon they turned sorrowful. "Excuse me?"

Tina shook her head. "How they managed to get away with staging that whole thing and covering up for the fact that it was all planned is beyond me, and I feel awful for those who lost their loved ones, those brave souls like your husband."

Aunt Emma stared at Tina, then down at the hand on her shoulder. She brushed it away, then turned around with a sad grunt and left.

Bryan stood behind her, startled, barely breathing. Had he really just witnessed that happen? Had his wife just said that? Or was it a dream?

A nightmare?

Tina turned to face him, then smiled. "Do you want to do the dance now? And show me what you've learned?"

Chapter 13

"I'M GONNA NEED A CREW HERE."

"What's that?"

Isabella shouted the words into the other end of the phone.

"I'm sorry," she continued with the same tone of voice. "I'm having a hard time hearing you. You keep falling out."

"I need a tech team," I said. "I need their room on the ship dusted, and I will probably need Luminol as well."

Isabella went quiet for a second. "You want to look for traces of blood? You think someone was hurt?"

"I want to be certain. Something is very much off here. There was money taken from the room."

"Really?" Isabella said. "That's odd. A burglary? Could a burglar have taken the kids?"

"Maybe they saw him?" I said. "They could have woken up while he was taking the money. He panicked and took them, or maybe even hurt them, then got rid of them. That is, of course, the worst-case scenario here."

"But then what happened to the mom?" Isabella asked.

"Maybe she was in there too? Who knows?" I asked. "I just know I need to secure any fingerprints or DNA before it is all gone."

"Yes, yes, of course," Isabella said. "I'll get you a tech team onboard the ship."

"I would prefer that they be American."

She sighed. "I can't promise that. You know this. We have to talk to the Bahamian authorities first and make sure they're willing to give us permission to send them in."

I rolled my eyes and groaned. Politics. Always in the way of getting things done. The real work.

"Then you better get on it," I said.

"These things take time," Isabella said, sounding tired.

"You're kidding me. They're American citizens. Three of them are missing. We suspect a serious crime may have been committed. That should be more than enough."

"The thing is, the ship is registered under a Panama flag," she said. "You're on a private island, and the crime happened at sea, closer to the Bahamas than the U.S. It's complicated. It's all about who is paying the bill."

I groaned loudly and rubbed the bridge between my eyes. "Listen. I don't have a lot of time here before people start to revolt against us. There has already been a fight, and the passengers are getting drunk. It's only a matter of time."

"Maybe stop serving alcohol?"

"Yeah, that will go over well. It's literally the only thing these people have left of their dream vacation—lying on the pool deck and drinking. If I take that away, they will burn down the ship; trust me. Just get me some people here who can go through the room, or I will pay for it myself. Bye."

Part II
SUNDAY 1 P.M.

Chapter 14

THEY HAD BEEN SEARCHING the waters since right after midnight, and Juanita Rolle was feeling beyond exhausted. She had been at home, finally sleeping after her newborn son had kept her and her husband up by crying for hours on end when she received the call.

Two children and their mother had gone missing from a cruise ship. It was feared that they had fallen into the water.

Juanita was the only helicopter pilot in the Bahamian coast guard, so she was the one they called first. The fact that her newborn had a fever didn't matter in this case.

But now that she had been searching the waters for more than twelve hours, she was anxious to go home soon. She desperately wanted to check on her kid and make sure he was okay.

Still, she felt awful for the poor children and their mother. The Atlantic Ocean was enormous, and their chances of being found were very slim. So far, they had found nothing, not even a piece of clothing floating on the surface.

"How long are we going to keep this up?" Lt. James asked. He and Lt. Williams were sitting in the back, looking out the window.

Finding a person in the ocean was rare. So often, Juanita had been called out on tasks like these, but only three times had she actually found the person, and they had all been dead. Most were jumpers from the ships, people committing suicide; others were capsized boaters who had been surprised by rough waters or bad weather.

But they were rarely alive—especially after this long.

"Have you heard anything?" Lt. Williams asked.

She shook her head. "Radio has been dead silent for the past half hour. I think we're all getting tired."

"We're not gonna find anything," Lt. James said. "It's too late. Might as well go back."

She wanted to. Boy, did she want to turn this bird around and go back to base, so she could go home to her baby.

Finally, the message came over the radio.

Stop the search.

They were giving up.

The boats were ordered to return, and so was the chopper.

Juanita sighed. At first, with relief, but then she was overwhelmed with sadness, unlike anything she had felt all morning. What was this? Was it because they were children? It was always harder when it was little ones. She had only experienced that once in her ten years as a helicopter pilot for the Royal Bahamian Defense Force. Was it because now she, too, was a mother? Was it maternal instinct kicking in? It felt like she wasn't ready to give up. Something inside her told her to keep going a little more.

Just a little longer.

Why? She didn't know. It was an instinct. A hunch, a feeling that drove her to continue, this time searching closer to the island where the ship had docked. They had told her to search the area further out where the ship had been before they were reported missing, but now she swung the bird around and tried to go closer to the coast.

Again, she didn't know why. Just a hunch, but she felt compelled to follow it.

"This is way too close to the coast," Lt. Williams said. "The ship sails with about twenty to thirty knots. They were reported missing at eleven forty-five, so if you do the math, that means they must be out further. If they are, in fact, in the water."

"I know, but I just gotta check this one area over here behind the big reef."

"There's nothing but crab traps out there," he continued.

Both her passengers groaned.

"You can't do this," Lt. James said.

"You're defying orders," Lt. Williams said. "We'll get in trouble too. Besides, I really want to go back.

She didn't listen to them and continued. "It's on the way back. Don't worry. They won't even know."

"It's your funeral," Lt. James said with a shrug.

"Hold on," Juanita yelled, then took a sharp turn. The two men in the back held onto the straps under the ceiling.

She continued toward the big reef, where tourists came to dive and snorkel. She passed it, then arrived at an area that rarely anyone ever sailed through except to check the crab traps.

"There's no way they're out here," Lt. Williams said. "It's too far to swim. Especially for small children. This is ridiculous."

"The stream," Juanita said. "Look at the stream going through down there. There's a strong one right below us that could have taken them or their bodies this way. It's coming from way out there in the deep ocean. My dad is a crab fisher, and he used to take me out here as a child. I know these waters like the back of my hand. Just go with it."

"Okay, as I said…."

"It's my funeral, I know."

Juanita bit her lip. This had to work. Being a female helicopter pilot in the coast guard, and the only female as well, was hard enough. She couldn't risk that they would lose their trust in her judgment.

She swung the helicopter toward the crab trap area, then

lowered it to see better. And that's when she saw it. It wasn't much —just the color red shining bright up at them from below.

"Look out the window, boys," she said. "I think we found something."

"I'll be…," Lt. James said. "I think you're right."

"Get ready," she said and approached it slowly until they couldn't get further down. She hovered above it. By then, they could clearly see that it was, in fact, a body—a body wearing a bright red shirt.

"I'm getting ready for you to be lowered down."

Chapter 15

"STOP IT RIGHT THERE; what's that?"

I was looking over the shoulder of one of the security officers onboard while he was going through the surveillance footage with me. I put my knuckles on the table and leaned forward.

"That's them, isn't it?" I looked at the pictures on my phone that the dad, Bryan McCarthy, had sent me of his family. He had taken them the day earlier while on the ship, so they were very recent. I looked back up at the screen in front of me. Then, I nodded. "Yes, that is definitely Becky and little Nicky at the ice cream shop up on the top deck. What time is this?"

"It says here that it was five thirteen p.m.," the officer said.

"That's when the children went for ice cream," I said and plotted it in my notebook. "Alone. That fits with what Bryan told us: he came back with Nicky from Nassau and found Tina and Becky by the pool deck. Then he realized that Tina had been drinking heavily all day and that she was sitting at the bar, then decided to talk to her. He sent the kids to get ice cream, so they wouldn't hear them fight. So far, everything he has told us has turned out to be true."

I sat by the computer and scrolled through the manifest, looking at pictures of all the passengers that were taken of each and every one on the day they boarded—even the children. I had sent it to a colleague at Quantico to get him to run background checks on every person—even the crew members. I knew it was going to take some time, which we didn't have a lot of.

"Okay, let's continue," I said. "The dad says that next, he spoke to the mom in the bar. Let's see if we can get footage of that. He also said they fought, and then he decided to take both kids to the cabin to get changed before dinner. He took them there alone after telling Tina to stop drinking and get her act together for the children's sake—she was scaring them. I want to check if that all fits with what he said. Please. Let's start at the bar on the top deck."

The officer started running the footage from the bar, scrolling forward until we could see Bryan approach Tina, then he stopped and ran it. We watched as Tina drank from her drink while Bryan walked up behind her. He placed a hand on her shoulder, and she looked up at him, then pushed the hand away. Then she ordered another drink and Bryan sat down next to her. They started talking. It seemed very calm initially but got visibly heated after a few minutes. Bryan was gesticulating, and Tina's body language was getting angrier. It was obvious that she was drunk at this point. She was shaking her head at him, trying to turn away from him, but he grabbed her shoulder and tried to force her to look at him. Then she pushed his hand away again while yelling something, visibly agitated. Bryan got up, threw out his arms, and said something. She didn't even react to it, just kept her back turned to him. He stood there for a few seconds, then tried again. He placed a hand on her shoulder, now with a softer look on his face. He tried to reason with her, but she wouldn't hear it. She wouldn't give him the time of day. Instead, she kept talking to the man sitting in the bar next to her, ignoring her husband completely. Finally, Bryan gave up. He said something else, then turned around and left.

"Okay, stop it there," I said and noted the time code. "Next, I need you to find the footage of him taking the kids to the room. He must have been in the hallways or stairs or elevators with them. And finally, I need to see the footage of them in the restaurant if you have that, or at least entering it and leaving it. That would be the last time anyone saw those children alive, except for their parents. Also, I need to know how long Tina stays at the bar and whom she talks to there. I need to talk to the guy sitting next to her in the footage we just saw and the bartender. Can you arrange that?"

"Of course," he said. "I'll have my people on it."

"Perfect." I wrote it on my notepad so I wouldn't forget when the door opened, and Captain Larsen entered. He looked very serious.

"What's going on?" I asked.

"I just got word," he said. "They found someone. A body. They pulled a body out of the water."

"No," I said, almost dropping the pen from my hand.

Chapter 16

THEN:

"She said what?"

"That nine-eleven was just a big hoax or something; I don't remember the words. It was my wedding day, a lot was going on, and I had a few glasses of champagne. You know how I get when I drink that stuff."

Bryan's brother Darryl went quiet on the phone for a few seconds, like he needed to digest this information.

"Okay, so if you had a little too much to drink, then maybe so did she," he said. "Maybe it was just a misunderstanding."

"Maybe," he said.

"Didn't you talk about this stuff when you were dating? Were there any red flags?"

"It's not like a sexy discussion topic. No, I never asked her about nine-eleven or anything like that. We talked about what we liked and didn't like, and she was so perfect. We both love pizza but hate Thai food. We agree on most stuff, almost too much."

"I guess you should have dug a little deeper, huh?"

"Easy to say now. But the worst part is that she said it straight to Auntie Emma's face. It was so embarrassing."

"Ouch. When did this happen?" the brother asked.

Bryan could tell he was driving in his car by the sound of the engine in the background. His brother drove an old truck that was very loud. Why he held onto that ancient thing was beyond Bryan's comprehension. It wasn't like he couldn't afford a new one, especially not since he had just got promoted at the company where he worked as an engineer. But the truck had belonged to their grandfather, and it held sentimental value.

"Right before the first dance," Bryan said. He peeked over his shoulder to make sure Tina didn't suddenly walk through the door and hear him talking. He had been thinking about this thing since the wedding, and frankly, it was a huge turn-off for him.

"I could barely dance and kept stepping on her toes," he added. "I was completely thrown off by it."

"No one noticed; I promise. They were all looking at the bride. And those who might have probably thought you were just a terrible dancer, which you are, little brother," he said, laughing. "Listen, I'm sure you just misunderstood her. Tina is a great girl."

He nodded, feeling silly. "Maybe you're right. I just can't stop thinking about it; you know?"

"That's understandable. How about you just ask her?" he said. "You are, after all, married now; you should be able to talk about these things."

Bryan nodded as he saw Tina's Land Rover drive through the gate to their house. "You're right. I'll do that. Talk to you later, bro."

As Tina walked through the door, he hung up and put the phone down. "Hi, honey. Whatcha' doing?"

"I was just on the phone with my brother."

"And what did he have to say?" she asked and put her shopping bag down on the Spanish tiles.

Bryan shrugged. "Nothing much. The usual. He and Bette are going on a trip to California next month."

"That sounds nice," she said. She walked past him, pecked him on the cheek, then went into the kitchen. "Gosh, I'm starving. Shopping always makes me so hungry. I'm gonna make a sandwich. Do you want something?"

He shook his head and approached her. "No, thank you."

She turned and smiled. "What's up with you lately, babe? You seem so pensive and distant."

He bit his lip, wondering if now was the time. He decided it was.

"Nothing much, just the usual stuff, you know, nervous about the game and all." He paused. "Say, there was something I was wondering about."

She grabbed some bread and put it on a plate.

"Mm-hm? And what is that?"

He felt his heart rate go up. He really didn't want to ask her this, but he had to know. Didn't he?

"That thing you said about nine-eleven?"

She paused, then turned to look at him. "What about it?"

"Did you really mean it?"

Chapter 17

"WHO IS IT? Which one is it?"

I yelled the words as Captain Anders showed me the fastest way to the bridge. I had never known there were so many secret pathways on a cruise ship, but he had explained that all the ships had them, so the crew could move from one end of the ship to the other without being seen by the passengers. There was a lot going on behind the scenes that the passengers didn't know anything about, and usually, they didn't need to. That was part of the charm of being on a cruise—that everything went as smoothly as possible, and passengers didn't have to worry about a single thing.

"I don't know," he answered, holding the door for me as we got to the bridge. I walked inside. "They didn't tell me. All I know is that the coast guard found a body and pulled it out of the water."

"They're bringing her here," a tall man in uniform said as he approached us. "I just received word."

My eyes grew wide. "Here? But that must mean that this person is...."

"Alive, yes," he continued.

I stared at him, barely blinking. "Is it one of the children?"

He shook his head. "We don't know yet."

"But, whoever it is surely should be taken to a hospital?" I said.

"They're bringing her here; that's all I know," he said, looking as puzzled as I felt. "They'll land on the helicopter pad in a few minutes."

"But, certainly, they're still searching for the other two, right? I mean, if one of them was found out there, alive even, then chances are the others are there too?"

"Yes, they're still looking for the two others, scanning the entire area out there."

"Good. That's good."

"We should inform Mr. McCarthy," the captain said.

"You haven't told him yet?" I asked.

"No. So far, you're the only one who knows. We informed you as soon as we received the message from the coast guard that they were coming."

"This is… all very strange," I said. "Where is Mr. McCarthy?"

"I sent for him," the tall man in the uniform said. "A crewmember is bringing him here."

Barely had he finished the sentence before the door opened, and Bryan McCarthy stormed in, a severely distraught expression on his face.

"What's going on? I was told to come here. Have you found them?"

I bit my lip.

"You have, haven't you? Oh, dear," he said and clasped his mouth. "They're… something happened to them, right? I knew it. Tell me it isn't bad news. Please."

"I… I think it's good news, actually," I said.

He stared at me, surprised. "What?"

"They pulled someone out of the water, and she is alive, apparently."

"Really?"

"Yes, they're bringing her here while still searching for the others in the same area."

He leaned against the wall next to him. "I… I can't believe it. I had almost given up hope of ever seeing any of them again."

"Well, I hadn't," I said and placed a hand on his shoulder. "Let's go."

Chapter 18

"CAN I get a plateful of those chicken nuggets?"

"Of course."

The young girl behind the counter wrote his order down while Travis looked at the menu hanging on the wall behind her.

"And fries, I need a lot of fries."

She smiled without looking up. "Sure."

"Does it come with drinks?"

"Do you have the drink package?" she asked.

"No, I don't. But I will need two sodas as well." He reached inside his pocket and pulled out the money he had taken from the room the night before. He glanced toward the casino entrance next to the sports bar he was in, ordering food. He never made it to the tables as he had planned. He desperately wanted to play Texas Hold 'Em. He still had the feeling that he was on a lucky streak and that he could win.

"I just need your room number," the girl said as she placed the boxed food on the counter along with the drinks.

"Oh, wait. I also need a sandwich. Do you have any with just ham and cheese?" he asked. "No mayo, please."

"Sure," she said.

She walked away, then returned with a sub that she wrapped in paper for him. Then, she smiled again.

"Will that be all?"

"Yes, that's good. Did anyone tell you that you have beautiful eyes?"

That made her smile even wider. "Thank you, sir."

He grabbed the food between his hands, then nodded. "You're welcome."

He left the sports bar, then walked past the gallery where you could buy tacky art and wondered who on earth bought that stuff. He crossed the bar where he had gotten a couple of drinks two nights ago when he won three hundred dollars at the casino. He went toward the elevator and decided to wait for one when a loud noise drowned out everything else, even the annoying music that was constantly playing everywhere to make them all feel good.

The loud noise seemed to be coming from outside the ship. Several passengers rushed outside on the deck to see what it was, and he followed. There, up in the air, hovering above them, was a helicopter with the Royal Bahamian Defense Force's emblem on the side of it.

Travis stared at it while his heart started to hammer in his chest. He found the stairs leading up, then rushed to the top deck. Here, he could see the helicopter approaching the ship's landing pad. He could also see something else. The FBI woman he knew was on board was standing there waiting for it to land, along with the ship's captain and the dad—that NFL player, McCarthy.

The helicopter landed, and the side door opened. Someone was rushed out of it, flanked by two men in uniform. Travis could barely breathe as he saw the face of the person.

He recognized it from the wallet when he had taken the money from the room the night before. In her wallet had also been her license, and he remembered looking at it briefly, thinking she was pretty.

It was the mom.

Chapter 19

I STEPPED FORWARD toward the woman that I felt like I had gotten to know over the past several hours but had never met. She had a blanket wrapped around her, and her eyes seemed confused yet determined.

"Mrs. McCarthy, I'm FBI Agent Thomas. You have no idea how happy we are to wel...."

She stopped; her nostrils were flaring. "I don't care. I want to see my children. Where are my children?"

"How about we step down to the bridge and have a talk?" I said.

She shook her head. "No. No talk. I have been sitting on that crab trap for hours, waiting to be found. I'm exhausted and dehydrated, but all that kept me going was the thought of seeing my children again. Now, you take me to them."

Uh-oh. This is going to be tough.

I forced a smile. "How about you come with me, Mrs. McCarthy?"

"I want to see my children," she said. "Are you taking me to see them?"

"I'm afraid I can't."

"And just why is that?" she was beginning to shake.

I exhaled, thinking I might as well get it over with. "Because they, too, have been missing since last night."

She stared at me. She wasn't blinking. Then, she shook her head. "No. No. Say it isn't true."

She turned her head and saw her husband, who was standing next to me and hadn't said a word, much to my surprise. Then, she snorted.

"What did you do?"

I sensed how Bryan McCarthy winced. "Excuse me? What did *I* do? What is that supposed to mean?"

She approached him, pointing her finger at him. The blanket was dropped to the deck. Everyone stared at them.

"You did this, Bryan, and don't you dare to deny it. You threw me overboard from the balcony of our cabin. What did you do to the children? Did you throw them overboard too? Huh? I bet you thought you'd never see me again, huh? Well, surprise. Here I am. Now, you tell me and everyone here what you did; do you hear me? Tell us—the truth, please. Where are the children?"

Now, it was he who shook his head aggressively.

"Oh, no, you don't," he yelled. "You don't get to do this. You don't blame me for this. You hurt our children. Now, *you* tell us what you did to them. Come on. Go ahead. Tell us."

They stared at one another like two cats, ready to fight, waiting for the other to lash out first.

"What do you mean what I did? I've been in that freaking water all night!" she said. "After you pushed me in from the balcony."

He shook his head. "I have no idea what you're talking about. I would never push you in. I've been worried sick about you and the children."

"Don't give me that," she hissed. "Like you don't know perfectly well what happened to them."

"I don't," he said, raising his voice. "But I know very well that you do. You're the only one who could have come into the room.

You're the only one with a key card and a motive. You did it to get back at me."

"Oh, that's rich," she said. "I'm the one with a vengeance here? Yeah, right. I can't believe you. He's lying through his teeth, and I hope you can all see it. He threw me in the water; I even have a bruise on my throat to prove it. He tried to strangle me first."

He snorted loudly. "You're the crazy one of us; that's for sure. Please, I hope you can see through this act. It's all a stunt."

"Take that back; I'm not crazy. Why do you always have to say that?"

"You're an alcoholic. She has been drinking heavily since we got here. Ask any of the bartenders. They'll tell you."

"Because of you."

"So, now, I made you drink?"

He grunted, annoyed.

"Don't give me that again. See what I have to deal with? You all hear and see this, right? This woman is crazy. No, it's more than that. She should have been locked up a long time ago. I tell you, she hurt our children; I know she did. She's just trying to get away with it. She's deliberately blaming me so that you won't think she did anything when we all know she's the only one capable of hurting two little children, her own children even."

"Don't you dare…." She lunged at him and slapped him. "Give me back my children, now."

He pushed her back hard. A crowd had gathered around us, and a gasp went through it. But Tina wasn't going to take this lying down. Once again, she leaped toward him, this time with her fist in front. I grabbed her arm midair, then stood between them.

"Everyone, calm down, RIGHT now."

They were both breathing raggedly and panting. I could tell they were both ready to rip the head off the other. I gave them the same stern look I usually gave my teenagers when they were fighting. That made them back off, even though it was very reluctantly.

"Now, we're all going back inside the ship to figure this out," I said with the same voice I used on my children. "In there, I will talk to each of you… separately. I will get your stories. You will get to say what you want to say. And you two don't come anywhere near one another. Do you hear me? I will not have this type of behavior when we're trying to save two innocent children—when we're trying to save *your* children."

Silence.

I placed a hand on my belt next to my weapon.

"Is that understood?"

They nodded.

"Yes."

"Yes, *ma'am*," I added, then shooed them back inside, keeping them at least six feet apart at all times.

Chapter 20

THEN:

"What kind of a question is that?"

Tina stared at Bryan. She had turned around after he asked the question, and a frown had grown between her eyebrows.

"What do you mean?" he said. "It's a question like any other question. I want to know if you meant it."

She shook her head slowly. "Why would you ask me if I meant it?"

"Because I'm curious to know; that's all."

She threw out her arms. "Of course, I meant it. Why else would I say it? I don't go around saying stuff to people that I don't mean. Do you?"

He swallowed, feeling his heart drop. He knew the answer before she said it, but part of him had still hoped she would tell him differently. She could say that she was drunk and didn't know what she was saying or something like that. But now that she was looking him straight in the eyes and saying this, he knew there was no way to explain it away.

She really did mean it. And she really did believe it.

"How?" he asked. "How can you believe something like that and even say it to my aunt who lost her husband?"

"Because it's the truth, of course," she said with a groan. "Don't tell me you believe in that lame cover-up story about the Arabian terrorists?"

He grimaced. "What?"

"Don't you know? Where have you been? It's all a cover-up. Most people know that by now."

He closed his eyes briefly to make sure he wasn't having a nightmare. He opened them again, and she was still there, holding the butter knife in her hand that she was using to spread the mayo on her sandwich.

"A what?"

"A cover-up."

"Can't you hear how crazy that sounds?"

She shook her head, remaining surprisingly calm. "It's not crazy. The truth is out there."

He grunted, feeling awful. How did he not know this about his wife? How had he missed this?

"Where did you even get that idea from?"

"There are plenty of videos about this online."

He stared at her, unable to grasp this. "You saw the planes, right? And the towers falling?"

She groaned. "Ugh, I'm not denying it happened. I know all those people died, and that is awful. I'm just saying that it isn't what they told us. There's a lot the government has been covering up."

He wrinkled his forehead. "Excuse me? Is that really what you believe?"

"Okay, so tell me, how is it possible for jet fuel to melt steel beams, huh?" she asked.

"What?"

"It's not. I can tell you that much. So, why did the towers fall? How did those huge steel beams melt? Because it was explosives that went off from inside the buildings, not the airplanes. And who planted those explosives, huh?"

"I… I have no…."

"No, you don't because you refuse to see it for what it is, just like most of the sheep in this country. The government planted those explosives and caused the towers to fall."

"But why, Tina? Why on earth would the government do that?" he asked.

"Isn't it obvious? Because they wanted to create a new world order."

"What on earth are you talking about?" he asked, baffled.

"Okay, then tell me, why did tower seven fall, huh? It was never hit by an airplane, yet it still collapsed hours after the alleged attacks. It contained offices of the CIA and the department of defense. You don't find that a little strange, huh? And then they just blame it all on the Arabs and send us to war against them, making sure no one asks questions. Even the media was in on it."

"Oh, really?"

"Oh, yes. There's no doubt about it," she continued. "There's even a clip online where a reporter from BBC News announces the collapse of Seven World Trade Center—on live TV—while the building is still visibly standing behind her. How did she know it was going to collapse? I'm telling you; it was a huge inside job, and the media was in on it."

He shook his head, rubbing his chin. This was definitely a side to his wife he hadn't seen before. The question was whether he could live with it.

"I see," he said and was about to leave the kitchen. He needed some time alone to do some thinking.

She stopped him.

"Hey," she said and forced him to look into her eyes. Her glacier-blue eyes that always made him forget to breathe. "Just because we don't see eye to eye on a few things doesn't mean we can't love one another, right?"

She walked up to him and grabbed him by the collar of his shirt. She pulled him closer until they were face to face. He could smell her perfume, and it made his knees soft.

"It's okay to have different opinions, Bryan," she said softly. "I won't hold your ignorance against you if you won't hold my awareness against me."

Her lips brushed against his, and he closed his eyes, wanting to kiss her so urgently. He was terribly in love with this woman, and when you thought about it, she was right. This was just a small thing they disagreed upon. It didn't have to ruin anything. They could just choose never to talk about it again.

It didn't have to become a problem.

He grabbed her head between his hands, then pulled her into a kiss. Her lips were so incredibly soft, and she tasted like honey. He lifted her and pushed her against the kitchen island, deciding to forget all about nine-eleven and Auntie Emma. After all, it was in the past, while his future was right here, between his arms.

Chapter 21

"I NEED you to listen to me. Please. I feel like no one believes me, but I am telling the truth."

I nodded, then pointed at the sofa behind her. "I will hear you now. Please, sit down."

They had given me an empty cabin on the top deck to talk to her in while Bryan was taken back to the captain's quarters, where I told him to wait for me, as I would speak to him later. He argued for a little while, letting me know that I shouldn't listen to anything his crazy alcoholic wife had to say, but then finally agreed and let me go.

"I'm the one you pulled out of the water, okay? I'm the victim here," she said, then sat down on the small gray couch. I handed her a water bottle, and she took it, opened it, and drank. I drank as well while secretively staring at the bruise on her throat. It sure did look like someone had been trying to strangle her.

I sat down in a small chair across from her.

"Okay, let me get your side of the story. Let's begin with yesterday. What happened? You didn't go offshore with your husband and youngest daughter but chose to stay on the top deck. Why?"

Tina breathed, agitated, and I could tell she was having diffi-culty calming down. I still believed we should get her to a hospital to make sure she was okay, but she refused when I mentioned it and told me she just wanted her children back. I couldn't blame her. I would probably have done the same if my children were missing.

"Take your time to gather yourself," I said.

She nodded and drank more water, then looked at her feet. A crew member had brought her some clothes from her room so that she could get out of her wet ones, and she had gotten dressed in the bathroom while I had a discussion with her husband, who insisted that I didn't listen to a word she said.

She nodded, then looked up at me. "We were fighting. I didn't feel like I was in the mood to go to Nassau with him when we docked there. I wanted to stay here and…."

"Drink?" I asked.

She raised her eyes and met mine. She was very obviously feeling guilty.

"I mean, we might as well be honest here, right?"

She nodded heavily. "Yes. I know it wasn't the smartest choice to make."

"Especially not since you had your oldest daughter with you?" I said.

She sighed. "I know. I know. But well… I was on a cruise. For once, I was on vacation, a family trip where we weren't with other players, investors, scouts, or agents—whomever they constantly have us meet up with to further his career. It's always about him; you know? His career, him, him, him. For once, I just wanted to be me. Does that make any sense? Between him and the children, I never have any time for myself."

I nodded and wrote it down. "I know how that feels."

"You do? Oh, good."

I smiled at her. I needed her to trust me, trust that I believed in her in order to get her to tell me everything. So far, she came off as pretty normal, and I wasn't lying when I said that I understood what she meant. Between my children and my work, I never had any time to myself, and I never felt like I was enough at either of those two.

"What did you two fight about?" I asked. "It must have been bad since it made you want to drink?"

Chapter 22

TRAVIS WAS PACING in his room. Back and forth, back and forth, while biting the inside of his cheek.

"What am I going to do?"

He said the words to his reflection in the mirror. The small feet in the bed weren't moving. The chicken nuggets had been eaten, the sodas drunk, and now all eyes were closed, and there was the sound of light snoring in the cabin. He looked at the jar of sleeping pills on the counter. He had only used one in the drink; that was enough. He didn't like doing it. But he couldn't risk questions being asked or noises making people suspicious as they walked by in the hallway.

This way, he had the silence to think.

The mom and dad were both on the ship now, and he heard from other passengers that they had been fighting, blaming one another for taking the children. That meant no one was looking in his direction. This was good.

The question was what his next move was going to be.

He thought about sending an email. But that was so easy to trace. Same with a call or a text. This was the FBI, for crying out loud. They'd find him in a heartbeat. No, it wouldn't work.

But how, then, would he get the message to the parents?

This McCarthy person had money—a lot of it. He could spare some—send some Travis's way. It wouldn't hurt him and would mean the world to Travis. He would be able to gamble without thinking about how much he spent. He could probably ask for a million dollars.

No, make that two.

Why not three?

Travis exhaled and looked toward the bed. So innocent when they were asleep, right? Little ones with their eyes moving behind the closed lids, their skin so young and fresh, their rosy red lips.

Travis had never wanted children himself. He was sure he would only mess them up like he was messed up himself by his dad's many beatings before he finally left them and never returned, not even when their mother died.

There was no way he would ever make a good father to any kid. He was never going to be able to take care of anyone. Heck, he could barely take care of himself, right? His sister always ended up bailing him out of trouble. He was always in some sort of money trouble.

But this time, he had hit the jackpot. Now, everything was going to change.

Maybe write them a letter?

The thought was invigorating; a good old-fashioned ransom letter wouldn't be traced to him as easily. He pulled out a drawer and found some paper and an envelope. He found a pen in his jacket, one they handed out for free, then sat down and started to write.

How do you write a ransom letter anyway? How do you begin? Dear ma'am? Or just ma'am, then a comma? No, just the last name.

Mrs. McCarthy,

"Yes, that's it," he mumbled to himself. He couldn't sound like a nice guy; then they wouldn't believe it.

He had never done it before, but he had seen many movies where they wrote those types of letters.

How hard could it be?

Chapter 23

"I SAW SOMETHING ON HIS PHONE."

"Something?" I asked. "What does that mean? Like, what did you see?"

I looked at Tina McCarthy sitting across from me. She was rubbing her fingers against one another, her eyes lingering on them while doing it. I preferred to look people straight in the eyes when talking to them. It was just easier to see if they were lying that way —if they were avoiding eye contact. The other things I looked for were excessive fidgeting, if the tone of their voice or speech pattern changed, or if they went into extreme detail.

"He had been weird about his phone ever since we left the house to come on the cruise," she said. "We were driving to the airport, and I wanted to play some music, and his phone was plugged into CarPlay. I grabbed it and opened it, but then I realized he had changed his password. I asked him why, and he didn't really answer; he just mumbled something that didn't really make sense. That's when I got suspicious. I asked for his passcode, and he wouldn't give it to me. I kept asking *why not*, and he didn't answer. I asked him why he was being so weird about it, and then he finally groaned and told me the passcode. I opened the phone and started to look through his music when a text message popped up, and I clicked it. It was a video. A beautiful woman was filming herself naked in front of a mirror."

She paused and rubbed her fingers, still not looking at me.

"Did you ask him about it?" I said.

She nodded. "I got mad and started yelling in the car. I asked him what the heck it was and who she was, and probably freaked out a little. He just told me I was scaring the kids and to leave it alone. I kept asking *who is she* and *why is she sending you this video*? And he said women do that all the time; it doesn't mean anything— because of who he is and all that. Being an NFL player and all, it's what comes with it. And I should see the kind of stuff some of the other players receive. He kept going on and on about how annoying it was and how he was scared that I would see it one day, and that's why he changed the passcode, but that it meant nothing; she was nobody, and he didn't even know her. So I asked him how she got his number, and he said he didn't know. These girls pass them around to one another, apparently. I didn't believe him, so I scrolled through his texts to see if he had texted her back, but he hadn't. There were just a bunch of videos and pictures of her and then small messages from her like 'thinking of you' and 'give me a call.' Stuff like that."

"But he hadn't answered her at any point?" I asked.

She shook her head. "I still didn't buy it, though. And that made him furious—that I didn't trust him."

"So, that's what you were fighting about?" I asked.

"Yes, I tried to believe him, but this voice inside my head kept telling me that he was hiding something. I couldn't let it go. I was so angry with him and didn't want to be around him. I just wanted to get drunk. I felt so betrayed. You must understand; I gave him everything. I have been taking care of him and his career for the past twelve years of my life. It's been all about him. And for him to… betray me like that… well, it hurt."

I nodded, thinking about my own ex-husband, and when I found out he had been cheating on me for the better part of a year, and now he wanted to be with her, leaving me alone with our three children after all we had built together. It was truly devastating and a wake-up call like none other I had experienced. I could understand her anger.

"That's perfectly understandable. And it would even explain it if you wanted to hurt him back by taking his children away from him."

She looked up, and our eyes met. She looked almost terrified. "Is that what you think I did? You think *I* took them?"

Chapter 24

THEN:

"So, did you ever ask her about that thing at the wedding?"

Bryan looked at his brother Darryl. They were standing on the porch outside. They were drinking beers while looking at the fifty-two acres of land by the house that Tina and Bryan had just bought. There were stables and pastures with horses, so Tina could pick up her riding again, something she desperately wanted to do. Bryan had bought the twenty-three-thousand square-foot mansion for her and for their future children to grow up in.

He sipped his beer, then nodded. "Yeah, but it's all in the past now."

"What do you mean?" his brother asked. "It seemed very urgent to you back when you called me about it."

"I was overreacting. So what if she believes in that stuff?" he said with a shrug. "She is entitled to believe what she wants, right?"

His brother looked at him with a scoff.

"What?" Bryan asked. "Are you gonna tell me there is nothing your wife says that rubs you the wrong way?"

"Well, this is a little more than that, don't you think?" he said. "It's a little more serious, at least to me it would be."

"I don't think so," Bryan said, hoping to close the conversation. "I love her enough to let her believe what she wants. I just don't want to fight about it; that's all."

Darryl nodded. "Fair enough."

He paused, then continued.

"Besides, now that the baby is coming, you've got a lot more on your mind," he said. "Congrats on that."

They clinked their bottles, and Bryan nodded. This was really happening. He was nervous about becoming a dad. His brother noticed his anxiety and placed a hand on his shoulder.

"You will be a great father."

"I'm just… is it too soon?"

"No. Not at all. You'll be fine."

Bryan exhaled, then drank more from his beer while looking in through the window. He could see Tina as she was setting the table with Darryl's wife, Bette. They were preparing dinner. The two girls were chatting and laughing, and that made him relax. His brother laughed.

"It's getting serious now, huh? Getting married, buying a house, and now, a baby. Does it scare you?"

He nodded. "Yeah, doesn't that stuff scare you? I mean, I want it, but still. It's terrifying, don't you think?"

"Nah. Not really. I mean, how hard can it be? Taking care of a tiny little baby? Just make sure you feed them, change them, and take them to the doctor for shots and stuff, and if they get sick."

Bryan scoffed. "Yeah, I guess you're right."

"And then when they're a little older, you make sure to send them to school. And just… you know, love them."

Bryan nodded and sipped his beer. Tina came out on the porch to them. "What are you two boys talking about?"

They looked at one another, then down at her bulging stomach. She smiled and touched it gently.

"I was just helping Bryan get over his baby jitters; that's all," Darryl said. "I told him that taking care of a baby isn't that hard. And to just make sure it gets all the shots and stuff, and you know, feed them and love them. And send them to school when they're old enough."

Tina stared at him, her smile waning.

"But our kids are not gonna get any shots."

Darryl laughed, then stopped himself when he realized she was being serious. He looked at his brother.

"What are you talking about?" Bryan asked.

She continued, "Yeah, they're not gonna go to school either. I will teach them here. At home." Then, she smiled. "Come on inside. Dinner is ready."

Chapter 25

"TO BE HONEST, I don't know what to think at this point," I said. "That's why I'm talking to you. I want to find those kids."

She nodded. "So do I. I'm really worried."

"Okay, so let's go back to yesterday. You were fighting and decided to stay on the ship with Becky while Bryan took Nicky and went to Nassau. How much did you have to drink?"

Her big eyes glared at me. "I... I don't know. Maybe four or five drinks?"

I wrote it down, then added that it was probably the double of that. People tended to lie about how much they drank, especially when talking to the police.

"I mean, I wasn't drunk. Maybe a little tipsy, but that's all," she added nervously. "I was still perfectly capable of taking care of Becky and keeping an eye on her, and I remember everything."

I smiled reassuringly. "It's not your drinking that we're investigating here."

She relaxed a little. "Of course not, but just making sure you don't think I'm some terrible mother who drinks while her kid drowns behind her back. I was keeping an eye on my daughter."

I nodded. "Okay, and then what happened when Bryan came back?"

"He came up to me in the bar and basically started going off about how bad a mother I was. I told him he was the reason I drank —because of what he had done. Then he went on and on about how he had already explained everything to me and why I kept bringing all that up when it was nothing. And then he told me I was *crazy as a bat*, which he always says about me, and he knows it drives me nuts when he says that. It just makes me so angry because there really isn't anything you can answer that won't make you sound like you actually are crazy."

"And then what happened?" I asked.

"He left. He took the kids back to the room. I finished my drink, then went down there as well to get ready for dinner."

"And was everything normal between him and the children when you got down there?" I asked.

"Not really. They were crying when I walked in, and I realized they were scared of me. He had basically told the children that I was insane and drunk and that they shouldn't listen to what I said, and that made me so pissed off. I started yelling at him that he was the one who was crazy for trying to turn my own kids against me, and if he thought I would let him do that, then he would have to rethink everything. Because my children are everything to me, they really are."

She placed a hand on her chest, and her voice broke as she said it. I believed her.

"I would never harm them, and the fact that he… that he would say such an awful thing, just… well, it made me really angry with him—even more than when I thought he had cheated on me."

"Still, you all went to dinner in the restaurant downstairs together? How did that go?"

"It was awful. The kids were whining and being impossible, and Bryan and I weren't talking to each other. It was just so… ugh."

She shook her head, annoyed, before adding, "It's just not something you want your kids to see, you know? They feel everything and know everything. I couldn't stand it. I had some wine, and then he started to go off again about my drinking and how crazy I was, and I just couldn't take it anymore. So we ate really fast, then went back to the room. It was the kids' bedtime at eight, and Bryan said he would tuck them in since I was apparently 'too drunk.' I let him get them in their PJs and read to them, and instead, I just walked onto the balcony and stayed out there with my wine, trying to shake this terrible day. At around eight thirty, they were sleeping."

"And then what happened?"

"He came out to me on the balcony, and we continued to fight. In the end, I couldn't take it anymore, so I left the room."

"What time was that?"

"Around nine."

"Where did you go?"

She looked down at her fingers. "I... I went to the bar on the top deck. There was a guy there who had talked to me earlier and wanted to meet me. I found him, and then I... went back to his room, where I... I slept with him."

Chapter 26

TRAVIS GOT out of the elevator, then rushed down the hallway. It wasn't hard to find the room they were keeping her in since two of the ship's security guards were standing outside, making it pretty obvious. Travis had heard from one of the crew members who knew his sister that they had put the husband in the captain's quarters, which was even harder to access. Plus, he wanted the mom to get the letter. She was the sentimental one; at least, he assumed so. She was a woman, and they were easier to persuade when it came to these things. She probably didn't care how much it would cost her.

As he walked down the hallway, he felt the sweat on the palm of his hand. He was holding the letter between his fingers inside his pocket. The two guards didn't seem to notice him at first, but when they did, they stopped him.

"Excuse me, sir. You're not supposed to be here."

He felt his face redden and touched the letter between his fingers again. He planned to pull it out and show it to the two guards, then let them know that he found it and thought it was important.

But now, as he was standing in front of those two men, he suddenly didn't know if this was the right way to do it.

"Is this… is this where they're keeping the mom?" he asked, stuttering.

"It's a restricted area," the security guard to the left said. "You can't be here."

"No… I know it's just…."

The letter felt almost like it was burning between his fingers. Should he do it? Was it too risky?

He lifted his gaze and looked at the security camera mounted under the ceiling. That little treacherous round thing was always spying no matter where you went. He was wearing a baseball cap for the same reason and didn't lift his face, so they couldn't actually see him if they looked at the footage.

It still scared him.

"It's just what?" the guard said. "You need to leave now."

"No… I was just… well…."

He paused. He couldn't find the words.

You idiot. Just hand them the letter. Say you found it in the bathroom some-where—or on the floor.

Travis felt panic spread all the way to his fingertips. No, this wouldn't do. It was too suspicious. They wouldn't buy it. And then he would have led them onto him. He couldn't have that.

Abort!

He smiled goofily and sensed how he almost shrunk in front of them. Or maybe they were growing taller. It was hard to tell; he suddenly felt very uncomfortable. His heart was beating so fast that he could hear it. His breathing had become ragged. It was too obvious.

Get out!

"I'm sorry," he said. "I think I went down the wrong hallway. I was supposed to be on the other side of the ship. I'll just…."

He said the words while backing up. The guards looked at him, eyes narrowing, foreheads wrinkled.

Or was that just in his imagination?

"I'll just be… going now."

Travis turned around with a small awkward chuckle, then started to walk away, taking long, fast strides, hoping to get out of there as quickly as possible. As he reached the end of the hallway and was about to turn the corner, he turned his head to see if they were watching him.

They weren't. One of them had pulled out his phone and showed the other something. Then, they laughed.

Travis breathed lighter, then rushed back into the elevator and waited for the doors to close. As they did, he pulled out the letter from his pocket and cursed his cowardice away.

Then, he had an idea. A brilliant one, too, if he had to say so himself.

Chapter 27

"YOU MUST UNDERSTAND THAT, at this point, I was really drunk and also… very angry and just sick of it all, you know? I'm not usually like this. I have never done anything like this before. Never."

Tina McCarthy coughed and drank water from her bottle. She finished it, then shook it from side to side. "Can I have some more, please?"

"Of course. Do you want some with electrolytes or Gatorade, perhaps?" She shook her head. I looked at her, a little worried about her condition after all that time in the water.

"Water is just fine."

I grabbed one from the fridge and handed it to her. She drank while I sat down again, hands folded.

"Listen, Tina. I'm not here to judge or in any way investigate your ability as a mother or determine whether you're a good wife or not. That is not my job. I am only here to find out the truth of what happened to your children."

She nodded, head bowed. "I know. I know. I just… I feel so guilty for what I did. It's not like me."

"I believe you. Nevertheless, I'm glad you told me. I'm going to need this man's name and the room he is staying in, please," I said.

She sighed and leaned back. "It's so embarrassing."

"I will make sure to keep it discreet."

"All right. His name is Frankie, eh, Wells or something like that; I'm not sure. He is on the fourth floor, in room 456."

I wrote it down, then nodded. "All right, we will check in with him later. Now, tell me what happened after you left his room. What time did you leave?"

She shook her head slowly. "I… I don't…." She stopped herself, lifted her gaze, and her eyes met mine. "No, wait a second; I think I did look at the clock in his room. It was around ten-fifteen, it said. I remember hoping that Bryan would be in bed by the time I got back to the room and praying he would be asleep so that he wouldn't ask me any questions."

"You went straight back to your room?"

She paused, then looked down at her fingers. "I may have gotten another drink. I needed something to calm me down. I went to the bar on my way there and had a lemon drop martini. I sat in the bar while drinking it, for maybe ten minutes, then took the rest of my drink back with me."

"So, around ten twenty-five, you left the bar and went back to your room?" I asked while jotting the times down on my notepad so we could check the surveillance cameras to see if her story checked out.

She nodded. "Yes, that sounds about right."

"So, we can assume you got back to the room at what? Ten-thirty?" I asked.

She nodded again. "Yes, that's pretty accurate."

"And you used your keycard to let yourself in, and then what happened? Were the children in the room?"

She nodded. "Yes, they were sound asleep when I walked inside."

I looked at her and wrote it down. This was the latest the children had been seen alive so far.

"Did everything seem normal, or was anything out of place? Were the kids fine?"

"I kissed both of them on the forehead like I always do. Then I looked at our bed and noticed that Bryan wasn't in it."

"Bryan wasn't there? Was he anywhere else, the bathroom or maybe the balcony?" I asked.

"No. Just me and the children."

"Did he text you where he was? Did he tell you anything about his whereabouts at this point?"

She shook her head. "Not a word. I couldn't believe he just left the children like that."

"You must have felt pretty awful at this point, thinking of what you had just done?" I asked, sipping my water bottle.

"I sure did. I felt terrible."

"Did you regret it?"

"Of course. I have spent years building this family. I wasn't ready to let it be torn apart like this. I did what I did because of what Bryan did to me. He cheated."

"It was revenge?" I asked.

"Sort of. I wanted him to hurt, so yeah, I guess so. This guy, Frankie, had hit on me all afternoon in the bar, and he made me feel wanted—like I was still good enough for someone. I haven't felt that way in a long time with Bryan."

"So, now you were even? Or did you still want to hurt him?" I asked. "Was it enough revenge?"

"I wasn't thinking about hurting him anymore," she said. "I regretted it and felt awful, but mostly for the children."

"It didn't feel as good as you had hoped? The revenge wasn't as sweet, or maybe it didn't hurt enough?"

Tina scoffed. "I know where you're going with this, and no, that is not when I decided to take the children to hurt him. I didn't kidnap them from their father because we had some fight."

"No one would blame you if that's what you wanted to do—if you wanted to keep the kids out of his life and take them somewhere

99

where he couldn't find them. Maybe even to protect them from all the fighting?"

She exhaled. "Gosh, this is tiring."

"I mean, I might have done something similar myself."

"You have children?"

I showed her four fingers.

"Four?" she said. "Oh, wow."

"My ex cheated on me, and I left with the children," I said. "I moved to another state with them. He wasn't too happy about it, but I needed to get away. I knew I couldn't stay and watch him start a new life with the woman he had deceived me with."

She shook her head. "Good for you. You shouldn't."

She paused again, then looked at me.

"Listen, I would be lying if I said the thought hadn't crossed my mind. Of course, it did. But the answer is no. I didn't take them. I didn't hide them somewhere from him."

"Okay, so what did happen?" I asked. "What did you do next? After realizing that Bryan wasn't there?"

"I kissed the kids on their foreheads and tucked their little bodies inside the covers."

"Was there a flat sheet?"

"Excuse me?"

"On the children's bed," I explained. "Was there a flat sheet between them and the duvet cover?"

She looked at me, surprised. "Yes. Why?"

I shook my head. "Continue."

"I grabbed a bottle of wine from the fridge and walked out on the balcony with the intention of drinking until I passed out. I just didn't want to feel all the pain anymore. I wanted to be numb. I wanted not to feel anything. Is that so terrible?"

She looked at me for reassurance. I gave it to her. I had come to learn that in interview situations, that was usually the best route to take—to make them feel seen and heard and not like there is something wrong with them. Feeling judged could make any person shut up, especially about touchy stuff that was hard for most to talk about.

"I guess that is probably a very normal feeling."

She swallowed. Her eyes were sad and filled with regret.

"I opened the bottle and poured myself a glass of wine while watching the ship move across the ocean, listening to the water move underneath it. It was so calming and beautiful. I remember thinking about my dad and how he always made me feel better when I was younger, and I decided I would call him in the morning and ask him what he thought I should do, even though I knew he would tell me to come home. Then I remember thinking about the time John Gerhardt cheated on me in eleventh grade and broke my heart right before I fell asleep."

"You fell asleep?"

She nodded. "Yes, I was deep into dreaming when I woke up, and I was being strangled from behind. I struggled to get free and panicked because I couldn't breathe, and that's when I passed out. The next thing I knew, I woke up in the middle of the dark ocean. Water was all around me, and nothing but darkness. I thought I was going to drown until I was somehow pulled by a stream, and my hand touched something made of metal that I grabbed onto and crawled up on."

"The crab traps?"

She nodded again. "Yes. I cut myself on them but managed to crawl up on one and stay there until the sun came back up. Then it became hot as heck out there, and I thought I would die of thirst and starvation. Just when I was about to give up, the chopper came over my head, and I was picked up. I was so thrilled with the prospect of getting to see my children again. It was all I could think about and the reason I refused to go to the hospital and told them to bring me here. The children were all I could think about."

She paused, then looked up at me with tears in her eyes.

"But then you tell me they aren't even here? Where are they? Where are my children?"

Part III

SUNDAY 3 P.M.

Chapter 28

TREVOR HOBGOOD WAS sick of being out at sea. It was boring enough, to begin with, and all of it was his wife's idea, but now they had been cooped up inside this ship all day without being able to leave, even though the ship had docked. With two children ages four and seven, it was really exhausting. His wife, Marie, thought so too, and she had thrown a fit at all of them just half an hour ago, screaming at him to take the kids somewhere—*anywhere*—just as long as it was away from her.

He had done so immediately. He couldn't blame her, really. The boys were a lot to handle, and the pool upstairs was so crowded that it was no fun. So instead, he had taken them to the ice-skating rink in the center of the ship. It was nice and cold on the bleachers where he was sitting with the youngest while the seven-year-old skated in circles on the ice, smiling happily and burning some of that energy he had been left with all morning. Trevor could finally breathe again. His wife got some much-needed alone time, and he would be rewarded for that later on. If not in bed, then at least with a happier woman by his side.

"Daddy, Daddy, look what I found!"

Trevor didn't look up from his phone. He was scrolling through his Instagram, seeing what his friends were up to, liking their pictures of fishing trips that he wished he was on instead. These cruise ships were like floating amusement parks—fun for the kids but not so much for the adults. At least not for him. Trevor preferred the great outdoors, hunting, fishing, or even camping. But that wasn't Marie's idea of a vacation. Especially not with the two young ones. She wanted them to try the slides and then lay by the pool, a cocktail in her hand.

And so Trevor had tried to give her all that for her birthday this year. How could he have known that two children would go missing and their vacation would be ruined? Now, all he could do was *like* and scroll while all his buddies showed their catch from the yearly fishing trip to Key West. It was the first time he wasn't there with them.

Boy, what he wouldn't give to be there right now.

"Daddy, Daddy, look!"

"Yeah, yeah, I'm looking, Jake," he answered without lifting his gaze from the phone. His best friend Mike had caught a tarpon as big as himself. Oh, how jealous Trevor was. He groaned and continued to scroll without liking the picture. He wasn't going to give Mike the pleasure.

"Daddy!"

"What?"

Trevor finally looked over at his four-year-old son, Jake, who had been playing further down the row of bleachers. Then he looked at what the boy was kneeling next to.

A wrinkle grew between his eyes.

"What's that, buddy?"

"A suitcase, Daddy," he said.

The boy tried to pull it, but it was too heavy. He had to let go, and it fell to the side, then sprung open.

Now, he had gotten his dad's full attention. This didn't look right.

Trevor got up. "Wait a second, buddy, don't...."

But it was too late. The boy had already looked inside and was pulling at the edge of the white sheet.

"Maybe you shouldn't...." Trevor hurried toward him. "Don't touch it, sweetie, please; Daddy is com...."

"Look, Daddy," the boy said, and Trevor did.

He stood there for a very long time, staring at the little boy's hand and the even smaller hand he was holding in his.

Chapter 29

"YES, I spoke to the guy, Frankie Wells, just about half an hour ago, and he confirms everything that Tina told me. She went looking for him, even though he didn't think he would see her again after he had seen her fighting with her husband at the bar on the pool deck. They went immediately back to his room. He said she left at around ten, and he just watched TV in his room, then fell asleep."

Isabella sighed on the other end. She had called for an update. She told me that some bad weather in Texas had delayed her plane, and she was stranded in Atlanta. She wasn't in a good mood.

"Gosh, I want this case off my shoulders," she growled. "The press is already calling and asking all kinds of questions. Luckily, you're far away in a place they can't get to easily. But it probably won't be long before they get some local helicopter pilot to fly them out there, or maybe by renting speedboats; who the heck knows? Just prepare yourself for them coming into the mix as well."

I stared at my computer screen in front of me, where I was going over the surveillance footage of Tina that the security officer had found for me. So far, it all confirmed her story. I blinked my eyes tiredly. I desperately needed some coffee to keep me awake.

"So, who is lying?" Isabella asked. "You have spoken to them both now. One of them must be lying."

"I... I have to admit that it's hard to say. Usually, I'm very good at seeing through people's lies, but these two... I don't know."

"What did Bryan McCarthy say to his wife's story?"

"He said he was nowhere near the room when she came back. He didn't try to strangle her and then push her in the water from the balcony."

"So, where was he? He left the children to look for her. Where did he go?" she asked.

"According to him, he searched for her in all the bars and on the outside deck. There is footage of him in several of those places, but not at the time that Tina says she was pushed in the water."

"And she's certain it was him who did it?"

"She claims it was, but... when I asked into the details, I realized she didn't see his face."

"In reality, it could have been someone else," Isabella said.

"Yes, I keep thinking that—what if they're both so busy claiming the other one took the children that they're not even thinking about the fact that there could be a third party involved? After all, there is money missing from the cabin."

"So, both might be telling the truth, and both might be innocent?" Isabella said. "Is that what you're saying?"

"That's what I am leaning toward right now, yes. But so far, no fingerprints or DNA was found that didn't belong there."

"This person could have been wearing gloves."

"It's still hard not to leave any evidence behind," I said. "Like hairs or fibers from clothes."

"True. But then again, the missing money could also be a diversion. You know, to make it look like a robbery gone wrong. It's been seen before."

"And the flat sheet is missing from the children's bed. That worries me."

Isabella went quiet. I could hear her breathing.

"Yeah, me too."

I sat there, staring at my screen when the door to the security operating room was opened, and the captain walked inside. He took off his cap and held it between his hands while looking at me, and that's when I knew.

My heart dropped instantly.

"I gotta go, Isabella," I said with a heavy heart, then put the phone down. My eyes looked into Anders', and his were filling. I shook my head slowly.

"Please. Say it isn't so."

Chapter 30

THEN:

"You can't be serious."

Bryan knew he was ruining the mood at their dinner with his brother and Bette, but he couldn't just sit there and pretend like she hadn't said those things earlier on the porch. He had tried to ignore it, which had worked for at least through the appetizer, but now he couldn't hold it back any longer.

"What do you mean?" Tina asked. "Can't be serious about what?"

Darryl and Bette both stopped chewing. All eyes were on him now.

"You don't want our kids to go to school?" he asked.

"I will teach them at home as a good mother should," Tina said. "This way, we will know what they're learning. God only knows what those teachers teach these days. I want to make sure my children are taught correctly."

Bryan stared at her, barely blinking.

"She's right, you know," Bette said. "There's a lot going on in the schools today that you don't want your child to be exposed to."

"Really?" Darryl said and looked at his wife. "You too?"

She shrugged. "Just saying."

Bryan shook his head. He drank from his wine, trying to wrap his mind around all this.

"Okay, so maybe I can accept the homeschooling," he finally said. "But why no vaccines? Don't you want them to be protected from diseases?"

Tina scoffed. "Don't you know that those things cause autism? Do you really want to expose your children to that risk?"

"I was vaccinated as a child; I'm fine, so is my brother, and so are you," he said.

"Maybe, but many childhood vaccinations have been linked to autism and other learning disabilities. And some of them are quite redundant—like chicken pox, for instance. I had chicken pox as a child, and I just got sick, then got well again. And research shows that getting the disease naturally produces way better immunity against the disease. Why do we need to vaccinate our children against a disease they can just go through? I'll tell you why— because some people make a lot of money from this. How would they make more money if we suddenly stopped getting them? What if, one day, the government decided to put mind-controlling substances in some vaccination that we all have to have? We won't say no because, *oh no*, if the government says so, then we have to do it. We're so trained to do everything we're told that we never stop to think for ourselves anymore. And that's how you become a sheep, Bryan. I don't want my children to be sheep. I want them to think and stand up for themselves."

Bryan stared at her. He wasn't blinking. Darryl and Bette had both gone quiet, too, and were simply staring at her. Her cheeks had gone rosy, and the vein in her forehead was popping out. Her eyes were wide open as she continued.

"And do we even know just how harmful the effects of the vaccines really are? Who keeps track of the numbers? The government. Why would they be honest about that sort of thing? The federal agencies who approve these immunizations are too close to the pharmaceutical industry if you ask me. I mean, if you think about it, then, of course, it has harmful effects. How is the immune system supposed to handle so many vaccines in a tiny infant? Why do they have to be injected with unsafe toxins right from the get-go? Do you know what is in those things? Formaldehyde, mercury, and aluminum. Can you believe they will inject that into a newborn infant who can't even say no? Why do we start their lives out by making them sick and weakening them when they should be building up their immune systems? It makes no sense. And I am not the only one who thinks so. A lot of Hollywood celebrities are deciding not to vaccinate their children."

"But won't we just begin to get all the diseases that have been eradicated?" Bette asked.

Tina scoffed. "That's another lie they'll tell you, but I read that it is commonly known in the medical world that vaccines aren't even responsible for decreased infections or eradicated diseases. Better sanitation is. Better hygiene makes sure fewer people get sick. I'm telling you; vaccines simply aren't worth the risk."

She rose to her feet and took the plate with the roast. Then, she smiled.

"Dessert, anyone? I made apple pie."

Chapter 31

¨IT WAS a child who found the suitcase. He thought it was a doll.¨

Captain Anders Larsen could barely keep himself composed. His voice was trembling, and he was obviously fighting his tears as he led me toward the ice-skating rink, where he said they found something.

A suitcase.

"His dad walked up to see what it was and realized...."

The captain held the door for me so I could walk inside the rink. The cold air hit me like a fist in my face. People had gathered behind the door, and security officers were telling them to stand back. I saw several crying faces, and it broke my heart.

I braced myself for what I was about to see.

"It's right over here," he said and pointed. "By the bleachers. I guess the suitcase was just put there, and no one noticed. The kid opened it and... well... then the dad came over and... then he called for help."

I nodded and followed him across the bleachers where a small group had gathered. One man was holding his child in his arms and another by the hand. His eyes were in deep shock as they fell on me. I had seen that look before.

I approached the red suitcase that was opened on the ground, and everyone around me backed up, giving me space to look. Inside the suitcase was a white sheet wrapped around the small body of a little girl. The right hand had fallen over the edge of the case and dangled lifelessly. I used my pen to swipe aside the sheet, so I could look at the face, then almost threw up.

It was Nicky.

I recognized her from the photos her dad had shown me on his phone. There was no doubt it was her. The two girls were very different in appearance. Where Nicky had blonde hair and light blue eyes like her mom, Becky had brown hair and green eyes like her dad.

I closed my eyes briefly to compose myself, then opened them again and looked at the tiny body in front of me that had been pushed inside the suitcase, even though it was slightly too big to fit.

I noticed finger marks on her little throat.

She had been strangled.

"Oh, dear God!"

The voice coming up from behind me felt like it was almost out of this world—so deep with horror and grief that it made me feel sick.

It was her dad. The security detail had brought him down, and now he was rushing toward the girl.

"It's my baby; it's my little baby girl," he cried, then knelt next to the suitcase. He was trying to grab her in his arms, but I had to stop him so he wouldn't destroy important evidence. A security officer tried to hold him back.

"Is it true? Is it her?"

Another person had entered and screamed with almost the same depth of terror, and I knew right away that it had to be the mom. I realized that bringing them down at the same time was an awful idea, but now it was too late. As Bryan saw Tina, he lunged for her, but the security officers held him back.

"Look what you did," he yelled, and it echoed loudly through the rink. "Look at what you did to our little girl!"

Ignoring him, Tina rushed toward the suitcase and looked inside, then clasped her mouth before falling to her knees.

"My baby! My poor baby!"

Tears rolled down her cheeks, and she looked at me for answers like I somehow could provide them or at least make her feel better.

But I couldn't take this away. No matter how badly I wanted to, I couldn't.

Then she turned her focus to her husband. He yelled at her:

"Don't give me that. You did this; you did this to her!"

"Me? How? How can you say such an awful thing?" she asked, her voice breaking. "You killed her. Don't you think I know it? You tried to strangle me, threw me overboard, and killed both our children. You thought I was dead, so you could blame their death on me. Say that I had killed them and then myself, am I right? You thought you'd never see me again. But I'm not letting you get away with this; mark my words. This is not over!"

Chapter 32

"I WILL GIVE you a good chunk of the money, okay?"

Travis looked at Elena. They were standing in the laundry room downstairs in the ship's basement, where she was leaving the towels and bedding she had changed earlier. The laundry room was right next to the morgue, and Travis knew Elena hated it down there. She had once explained to him that all cruise ships had a morgue in case someone passed away onboard. The cruise ships hosted a lot of elderly people, so it happened from time to time. She had shown it to him once. It was nothing but a freezer with room for three bodies. Some ships had bigger ones that could hold more, but not this one. Once she had heard a story of one of the ships, when they ran out of room, and there was someone who died, they put him in the freezer with all the meat, but she didn't know if that was just a story.

Elena bit the inside of her cheek. "What kind of money are we talking about here? A lot?"

He nodded. "We're talking about a future where you will never have to go to work again. That kind of money."

"How much?"

He looked around like he was afraid someone was listening to their conversation. But the washers and driers made such a loud noise no one would be able to even if they were in the room with them.

"I'm asking for two million." He smirked as he said it.

Her eyes grew wide. "Dollars?"

"Yes. Of course."

She narrowed her eyes. "And just how much are you proposing I will get of that?"

"Well, technically, I will be doing all the work; you only have to do this one little thing for me, so I can't give you half, but maybe let's say… ten percent?"

She shook her head and crossed her arms in front of her chest. "That's two hundred thousand. Nope. Not enough."

He exhaled. "Okay, then, five hundred thousand. You could buy yourself a house somewhere."

"I want eight."

"Eight hundred thousand for doing one little thing?"

"You haven't even told me what it is yet, or what you're doing, but I have a feeling it must be dangerous and criminal, or else you wouldn't be talking about this much money. So, yeah, I need a good cut of it. I'm sure you can't do it without me, can you? I mean, I could just walk away now and then…."

"No, no, please. I need your help with this."

"Should we say eight?"

He threw out his arms. "Seven-fifty, okay?"

She smiled. "We have a deal."

They shook hands.

"I would have settled for six, just so you know," she continued, mocking him as only a sister could.

"Yeah, well, I would have given you half, so I guess we're even, huh?"

She threw a towel at him. "You moron."

He laughed and caught the towel in the air. She smiled. He was happy to help her get out of this life she was living—cleaning up after people day in and day out. It was beneath her. He wanted her to get a shot at a better life. Maybe even have a family, have children. She deserved it.

"What do you want me to do?" she asked.

Chapter 33

I SEPARATED the parents and had the security officers take them back to the rooms they were in earlier. I told them to clear people out, and so they did and locked the doors to the rink. I was freezing, I knew I was, but I could barely feel it. I stood for a few seconds, composing myself, before I grabbed my phone and called Isabella again.

"Please, tell me you have good news," she said. "I need it."

I went quiet. I was fighting my tears while staring at the girl in the suitcase. It was just too much, especially when I had a toddler at home. My heart couldn't take it.

"Oh-oh," she said. "Good news doesn't start with silence."

I sniffled and tried hard to pull myself together, but I still couldn't speak.

"I take it you found them," Isabella said with a heavy tone to her voice.

I took a deep breath and bit my cheek to get my act together. Then, finally, I spoke. "Just the one girl. The youngest."

"The three-year-old?" Isabella said. "Geez, Eva Rae, I'm sorry, that's… oh, dear Lord… that's awful."

I nodded while letting a few tears escape my eyes. I had never believed in bottling up emotions when they were in their place. This was sad. This was very sad, and it was okay to feel that.

"I was right about the flat sheet."

"She was wrapped in it?"

"Yes," I said in a small voice. "Looks like she was strangled first, though."

"And the other girl?"

"No sign of her. At least not yet. I'm gonna need to have the ship searched by people who know what they're doing. I'm gonna need some help here. A lot of help, please."

"Naturally. It just became a homicide. That changes everything. Let me know what you need," Isabella said.

"I need a crew. Full-blown tech crew and I need it yesterday. And not some Bahamian crew who has no idea what they're doing. I want the best we've got. I want to catch that bastard who did this more than anything."

"Okay. I'll get a crew for you."

"They have to be good; do you hear me? Really good."

Isabella sighed. "Of course."

I bit back my tears. "I will also need agents here to block all the entrances. And I will need to interview each and every freaking passenger, so I don't miss anything."

"That might be hard. Keeping all those people from leaving? We've already kept them way longer than they're happy about."

"I don't care. Whoever did this to this poor little girl is somewhere on this ship. No one leaves until he is found."

"Geez, Eva Rae, that's almost four thousand people. We can't do that."

"The bastard put her in a suitcase, Isabella. A suitcase."

She went quiet for a few seconds, and I could hear her breathing heavily. I think she was crying.

"Do what you have to do, Eva Rae," she said. "Whatever it takes."

Chapter 34

THEN:

After their first child was born, years went by, and Tina didn't get pregnant, even though they tried endlessly to have another one. It tore hard on their marriage, and Bryan often listened to Tina crying in the bathroom alone at night when she thought no one heard her.

Bryan found it difficult to look into her eyes when he came home at night because of the deep sadness in them. It scared him. The sadness soon grew into resentment, and she started to blame him for the lack of more children in their lives. She always wanted a flock, she told him, but his swimmers weren't doing their job.

"It's all the pesticides and chemicals in our food," she declared one day, and from then on, all they ate was vegan and organic. Bryan didn't mind; he would go along with anything that made Tina happy at this point. But he did find himself avoiding coming home, or he'd go for an extra-long drive in his truck after practice. He enjoyed being away when they played games, even though he did miss both his wife and daughter a lot. He just found it too hard to look at them and know he had failed them. Their daughter Becky wanted a younger sibling to play with desperately and asked about it almost daily. And Tina would give him that look when she did, the one that felt like a punch in the stomach.

Like he wasn't man enough.

Sometimes, they would even fight about it; those were the worst days. They often happened after she had taken a pregnancy test and realized she wasn't with child or after she went to the bathroom and found out she was on her period. Those were the worst days, and he dreaded them more and more every year that passed. One day, seven years after the birth of Becky, he knew it was about time for her to get her period again, and he decided he wasn't going to go home after practice. Instead, he went out with his brother and had a few drinks. They weren't usually allowed to drink just a few days before a big game, but he didn't care much for once. He needed to drown his sorrows in something, so he chose beer.

"I don't know if we're going to make it," he said to his brother after his third beer. "I know I've said so before, but this time, I mean it."

His brother had four children within the past few years and looked at him with exhausted eyes, then laughed.

"I'm not sure Bette and I will either, but for entirely different reasons. It's a madhouse at home, and she is always yelling at someone. I am so happy when I get the chance to get out every now and then."

"I don't know what to do anymore. It's like there's this gap between us that she expects me to fill, but I can't because only another child will be able to. It's all she is focused on."

They were sitting in silence when both of their phones rang. Seeing that it was both of their wives, they didn't pick up. Instead, they ordered another beer. As it became late, and Bryan still didn't want to go home, they snuck into Darryl's house and went into the basement, where Bryan slept on his couch. The next morning, he woke up to the sound of children screaming, rushed out the door, and took a cab home. Tina was in the kitchen when he came back inside. He felt awful.

She didn't look at him.

"Where have you been?"

"At my brother's; listen... I'm sor...."

"You better be. I had dinner ready for us and everything. I waited all night for you to come home."

He looked at the dining room table. The food was still there; she hadn't cleaned up. She had made lasagna. On top of it, placed in the cheese, was a pacifier.

He turned to look at her with a light gasp.

"What... are you...?"

Finally, she looked at him, and a smile spread from ear to ear. She nodded, tears springing to her eyes.

"I was so looking forward to telling you."

"For real? We're having a child? We're having another child?"

She nodded again, and he grabbed her in his arms, lifted her in the air, and spun her, laughing. She squealed, and they kissed as she slid back down in his arms. A huge relief jolted through his entire body as he realized that, finally, everything was going to be good.

Finally, they were going to be happy.

Chapter 35

"THINGS JUST GOT VERY SERIOUS HERE," I said and sat down. I had to restrain myself a little in order not to scare him away. I was angry at this point. Seeing that little girl in the suitcase almost made me lose it. Still, I needed him to trust me to get him to open up.

Bryan was on the couch in front of me. His bloodshot eyes looked up at me. He had been crying. I put my notepad in front of me and sighed. This was really rough on all of us.

"Listen, I know it's a tough time right now for you and your wife; I get it. You just lost a child, and we still don't know where her older sister is. But I need some answers. It's time. One of you is lying, or maybe you both are. Your wife says you tried to strangle her, then pushed her into the water. She also says she believes you killed the children afterward. They were still sleeping when she went out on the balcony. I know we've been over this before, but now we have a body. The forensic team is examining the body of your three-year-old daughter now at the ice rink. They will find out if you killed her. It's time to be honest with me here. Was it just too much? Did it become unbearable?"

He stared at me, then shook his head. "I just lost my daughter, and the other is missing still. And then you come here, and… and ask me these stupid questions over and over again?"

"As I said, I know it's rough, but we gotta find out what happened. People snap. It happens. It was an accident, right? And then you had to get rid of the bodies. You're human. You panicked."

He scoffed. "You people are unbelievable."

"What do you think they're gonna find when they examine Nicky?" I asked. "Just tell me what happened, Bryan. We're going to find out anyway. Maybe you can help me find Becky? Did you hide her body on the ship somewhere too?"

"What are you talking about?"

"The suitcase. It had your nametag on it. It was one of yours. There are only three suitcases in your room; one is missing—the one we found Nicky in. But my question is, what did you do with Becky? She was too big, right? She couldn't fit in one of your suit-cases. What did you do with her body?"

He shook his head again.

"You believe her, don't you? You believe that crazy woman over me?" he said, almost hissing.

"She's your wife; why do you say she's crazy?"

"Ask anyone who knows her. She's insane," he said, pointing his finger at his temple. "Mad as a bat."

"Okay, then explain to me why she's the one who nearly died. Why does she have marks on her throat? Why did she end up in the water and almost drown? While you sit here unharmed?"

His eyes were almost manic as they stared at me in rage. "I don't know, okay?"

He got up and started to pace back and forth, throwing his arms out. "Maybe she did it to herself. Maybe she killed the chil-dren, then tried to commit suicide? Have you thought about that?"

"Would someone who tried to kill herself fight for her life all night long?" I asked. "Would she cling to a crab trap for hours in the scorching sun just to return to her children if she knew they were already dead? If she knew that she had killed them?"

He stared at me with a grunt. "How am I supposed to know? I don't know how her brain works or what her motives are. Why are you asking me these things? Ask her instead."

I observed him, scrutinizing his every move. He didn't strike me as someone who was lying. There wasn't anything in the tone of his voice or the way he answered me that told me he wasn't telling the truth.

Maybe he was just very good at hiding it.

I nodded. "I will. Later. But right now, I'm asking you."

I waited a beat to let him compose himself before I continued.

"Did you try to kill your wife? Did you try to strangle her, throw her overboard, and then go inside to kill the children? I want you to think about your answer here. This is your chance to tell me the truth. Lying is hard, and it tears you up. Accidents happen. Anger sometimes gets the best of us, and then we act without thinking. You were in a fight. It's perfectly normal to want to hurt each other. Maybe you didn't mean to let her fall overboard? Maybe the kids woke up and saw you do it, and you had no other way? You had to get rid of them? It happens, Bryan."

Bryan sat down and hid his face between his hands. He was making groaning sounds.

"This is the worst nightmare...."

"I know, it is," I said, trying to sound as sympathetic as possible. I wanted him to feel comfortable with me—enough to admit what had happened. "It can end here if you just tell me the truth."

He shook his head, then lifted his gaze and looked directly into my eyes. He spoke through gritted teeth.

"This is the last time I'm gonna say this. I didn't try to kill my wife, and I didn't kill my children."

"Then, who did, Bryan?"

"My wife did it. Go ask her."

I got up with a deep sigh and walked out of the room. I shook my head as I met Dana, the leader of my new team that Isabella had sent me from Miami. She was small, even shorter than me, had short pixie-cut hair dyed blonde, and it was apparent that she worked out a lot. A tattoo of what looked like a rose peeked out underneath her sleeve.

"He remains steadfast. He didn't do it, he says."

"I don't believe him one bit," she said.

I grabbed the thermos, poured myself a cup of coffee, and then looked at her.

"I need a medical expert to look closely at the wounds on Tina McCarthy's throat. I need them to tell me if they could have been self-inflicted."

"Of course. We will take care of it right away."

"Perfect."

I was about to leave when Dana stopped me.

"By the way, Director Horne called while you were in the room. She's been trying to get ahold of you. You should probably call her back asap."

Chapter 36

"YOU WANT ME TO DO WHAT?"

"Hand this letter to the mom."

Elena looked at Travis, her pretty brown eyes questioning him. "You can't be serious? We're talking about the mother of the two missing children?"

"Yes."

She lifted both her eyebrows at the same time. "The one who was pulled out of the ocean?"

He nodded. "Yes, her. Now, just do it, please."

Elena swallowed. She wasn't ready to let this go yet. There were more questions. "Why?"

"Does it matter?" Travis said. "I will give you seven hundred and fifty thousand, remember? That means not asking any more questions."

"But, Travis… this seems… I need to know what the letter says, no?"

He shook his head. "The less you know, the better it is for you—for your own protection."

"Okay, I guess that makes sense in case something goes wrong," she said, looking down at the letter in her hand.

"You have access," he said. "You have the key to her room and can let yourself in. Tell the security officer you're cleaning the room. Then, hand it to her as soon as you're inside."

"No. I can't do that," she said, handing the letter back to her brother. "They'll come after me, asking me questions."

He placed it back into her hand. "You say you found it in a bathroom, one of the public ones, and you thought you would give it to her. Just bat your eyelashes a lot, and they'll believe you."

"Why not give it to the police, and then they can give it to her?"

"I want to make sure she reads it. They might keep it from her, so she won't even have a chance."

Elena sighed; she gave the letter back to him again. "I don't know, Travis. This is… it's just…."

"Money enough to buy yourself a house," he said luringly. "No more having to clean up other people's messes."

That made her stop talking. She stared at him, and he could tell she was thinking about it. She just needed one more little push.

"Maybe you could buy yourself a pair of Jimmy Choo's like you've always wanted. Remember the red ones we saw in that magazine once?"

"Give me that," she said and pulled the letter out of his hand.

"That's my girl," he said and smiled. He kissed her forehead, then whispered. "Now, go before anyone sees us together."

She took off, grabbed her cart, and pushed it down the hallway with the letter tucked inside her front pocket. As she was out of his sight, she stopped, pulled the letter out, and looked at it.

Then, she did the one thing she wasn't supposed to.

She opened it.

Chapter 37

I WALKED DOWN THE DECK, phone clutched against my ear, calling Isabella. She picked up right away. The sun was burning my face, and I began to sweat even before we had said our hellos. The paradise-like island was right in front of me, with its white beaches and blue water. It was strange to see the island so deserted. Only Royal Bahamian police boats were docked next to our cruise ship, and uniformed men were walking around.

So much for paradise.

"Eva Rae, glad I caught you."

"What's up?"

"Our agents went through the manifest, and a few names raised red flags. I think they're worth checking out."

"Yes?"

"Actually, there are three people onboard with priors. You might want to talk to all three of them."

"Okay, what are their priors?"

"The first one is Emilio Vanquez," she said, and I could hear her tapping on the keyboard of her computer. "I'm sending you all his info as we speak."

"What did Emilio do?" I asked.

"Petty theft—stole a couple of cars a few years ago, then later in 2015, he did time for robbing a convenience store in Idaho."

"Okay, we'll have a chat with him. What else?"

"Then we have Gerard Hutcheon, a sixty-three-year-old male from Philadelphia. This one is interesting if you ask me."

"I see, and why?"

"His prior stems from trying to buy someone's child in the parking lot of a Walmart. Twice."

My eyes grew wide. "Really? That's so odd."

"I know, but that raises a red flag for sure."

"Indeed," I said and wrote his name down next to the first one, then made a mental note to take a closer look at this guy first. "A huge one. What else?"

"Elena Gasgarth. She's a member of the cleaning crew."

"I see; that sounds interesting, too," I said. "She has access to the rooms."

"Yes, exactly."

"And what is her prior?"

"Kidnapping a minor."

"Really? That's very interesting."

"I thought so too."

"This is very good, thank you," I said.

"Any sign of the second girl?" she asked.

"Not yet. But no other suitcase is missing from their room, so I guess we shouldn't look for one. I just don't know where to start searching. This ship is the length of three football fields and has nineteen decks. There are five thousand people here, including the crew. A needle in a haystack would be way easier."

"Find her, please. Find her fast, and then lock up this bastard."

Chapter 38

THEN:

The second pregnancy was very different from the first. Because of the hardship of getting pregnant, Tina was more anxious than the first time around. She had become terrified of losing the child after two miscarriages in the past seven years. She spent most of her time in bed or on the couch, a laptop on her knees, while Bryan took care of their oldest, Becky, and everything else around the house. He didn't mind. On the contrary, he wanted to help as much as possible so that she could rest and focus on growing the small new life inside her.

He would do anything.

But as the days and months passed, Bryan got more worried about Tina's mental state of mind than her physical condition. She seemed to be constantly on her phone or computer, watching and reading stuff, and often, he could barely get her to look up. Their daughter Becky, who was seven then, was craving her mother's attention but only got it rarely.

One night Bryan woke up at two a.m. He blinked his eyes, wondering why it was so light in the bedroom. He turned around and saw his wife sitting up on her side of the bed with her laptop on her knees. He stared at her as the blue light hit her face, and her eyes were manically moving. She didn't seem to be blinking at all, and her lips were mouthing words that he couldn't make out.

What is going on with her?

Concerned, he sat up in bed, thinking she might notice and look at him, but she didn't. She kept reading, her eyes scanning page after page. He watched her for a few minutes as she started a video and listened to it through her headphones, small gasps escaping her lips.

"Honey?" he said.

But she didn't react. He tried again.

"Sweetie?"

She kept staring at the video, and Bryan felt nervous. Was she having a nervous meltdown or something? Was this normal behavior for a pregnant woman? Maybe it had to do with the hormones.

"Are you okay?"

He placed a hand on her shoulder, and finally, she reacted. With a loud gasp, she turned to look at him. She took off her headphones.

"Sweetie, why are you awake?" she asked, sounding concerned. "You should be sleeping."

"Why are *you* awake?" he asked.

"I couldn't sleep. The baby keeps kicking and moving around."

"But the baby needs sleep, too," he said. "And you need the rest."

"I can sleep whenever she does," she said, with a light laugh, holding her protruding belly with both hands.

"But shouldn't you maybe put the computer away? What are you watching?"

"Oh, just some videos," she said. "Stuff that interests me."

"I feel like you're on that thing all day long," he said. "Can't you put it away?"

She closed the lid and looked at him.

"You're kidding me right now?"

"What?"

"I can't believe you," she said. "You're so controlling that you're now trying to stop me from educating myself? What are you afraid of? That I might shape an opinion of my own?"

He felt suddenly awful and shook his head. "N-no, that's not what I meant."

"Then what did you mean?"

"I thought that maybe it would be great to spend some time with your family, Becky and me, instead of the computer or your phone. We barely see you and miss you very much. That's all."

She scoffed. "No, that's not all. You're trying to tell me what I can and can't do. What I am allowed to watch and read."

"No, I am not."

"Yes, you are. You're literally just telling me not to watch this, to put the computer away."

"But that's only because...."

"Is it really that frightening for you?"

"Frightening—what do you mean...?"

"I see what it is," she said, pointing her finger at him. "I see straight through you. You're scared I won't be your adoring little wife anymore, right? That I won't look at you while batting my eyelashes, being oh so impressed with you whenever you share some wisdom at the dinner table? That you won't be able to mansplain everything to me?"

"Mansplain...?"

"Are you scared that I will be smarter than you?"

He wrinkled his nose. What on earth was she talking about? He didn't understand anything.

"No, that's not it at all," he said, feeling terrible. How could she think this of him? "You can watch anything you want. I just miss you."

She bit the side of her cheek for a few seconds, then opened the laptop's lid again.

"I still think you're trying to control me. But I won't let you. You might as well give up."

He stared at her as she opened another video and started to watch. He was unable to grasp what had just hit him. Was she right? Was he just trying to be controlling? He remembered how his own dad had been around his mom. He was always telling her what to do and even what to wear. Bryan had sworn he would never become like him, and his marriage wouldn't become like theirs. Was this just a part of him that he wasn't aware of? Was he acting like a controlling husband?

Was he becoming his father?

The thought was sickening.

Chapter 39

"GERARD HUTCHEON?"

The tall man in the white T-shirt and white beard looked down at me, surprised when seeing the badge I was holding up. I had knocked on the door to his room, hoping he was in there and not somewhere else on the ship. Most passengers had grown tired of being in their rooms now and were frequenting the stores, bars, or the pool upstairs. The crew was putting on shows in the middle of the mall area to keep people entertained, and they were showing a movie at the pool deck. Yet it was getting harder and harder to keep the anger down, were the reports that came back to me.

I was running out of time.

"Yes?"

"Eva Rae Thomas, FBI, can we come in?"

Dana was with me, as I didn't want to do this alone. She had sent Kent Black, the medical examiner, to take a closer look at Tina McCarthy's bruises while we checked out the few passengers that had raised red flags during the background check. The first guy, Emilio Vanquez, had been quick since he had a watertight alibi for the entire night before. He was in the detention cell of the ship for fighting in the casino onboard the night before. He was still detained and visibly very hungover when I approached him.

Gerard shrugged but had a concerned look on his face. "Sure."

He made room for us to enter, and we walked into his room. It was one of the smaller staterooms downstairs with no windows. I always believed those were too claustrophobic for me and wondered who could stand to stay in one of those. But they were cheaper than the others. His suitcase was on the floor, clothes spread around it and on the bed. I scanned it quickly, and Dana checked the closets, bathroom, and the compartments under the bed.

Then she shook her head.

No sign of Becky.

"What is this about?" he asked, rubbing his fingers together—a sign of anxiousness and something to watch out for. He noticed that I was looking at it, then stopped. Seconds later, he started to pick at his nails.

I showed him the picture of Becky from my phone. "We're looking for this girl. I'm sure you have heard?"

He shook his head. I gave him a look, and he changed his demeanor.

"I mean, I have heard that two girls have gone missing, but…."

"Have you seen either of them?"

He shook his head. "No. Never seen them before."

"Can you guess why we're here?"

He exhaled, still picking at his fingertips and nails. "I can guess. It's because of what happened in Philadelphia, right? At Walmart?"

I nodded. "Could you maybe tell us more about it?"

"What do you mean?"

I shrugged. "Why did you do it?"

He ran a hand through his sparse white hair. "Listen, I spent three years on the inside for that. I paid my dues. You can't come here and ask me about this just because I once, many years ago, did something…."

"You haven't tried to buy any little girls since?" I asked, ignoring his little rant. I had heard it all before.

His eyes wandered. I noticed that they landed on his phone on the table next to the bed.

"No."

"You offered a hundred grand for these girls you tried to buy. What were you going to do with them?"

He shook his head anxiously. "It was just a joke."

"Really? Twice? You made the same joke twice?"

He was sweating now, his eyes wandering to the phone again. I pretended like I didn't notice.

"Yeah, well…."

"Did anyone find it funny?"

"I guess not."

"Did you want to buy Becky and Nicky too, or did you just decide to take them?" I asked.

"I didn't touch them. I swear," he said.

Again, his eyes wandered toward the phone. This time, he noticed that I saw him do it. I nodded to Dana to grab it, and she did. The sight of her holding it sent waves of panic through the guy.

"So, if I look through the contents on your phone, I won't find anything incriminating on it?" I asked.

He looked at me, then at her holding the phone. I could tell he was debating what to do next. Then, before I could react, he sprang for her. With great force, he pushed her against the wall and grabbed the phone from her hand. He was a big guy, and Dana was tiny—his weight looked like it would crush her, and her eyes rolled back in her head. I shrieked and went for my gun, but I wasn't fast enough.

Gerard stormed for the door with the phone in his hand while I rushed to check on Dana.

She had fallen to the floor.

"Are you okay?" I asked.

"Don't mind me," she said, gasping for air as it had been knocked out of her lungs. "Go after him."

I scoffed and helped her get up. "I just wanted to make sure you were okay. Are you hurt?"

"I'm fine." She coughed, then nodded toward the door. "Go ahead. Catch the bastard. I'll catch up in a second."

"We're on a ship," I said. "There's nowhere he can go. Even if he jumps in the water, we'll be there to pick him up. He won't make it far."

I grabbed my radio and sent out a search for him to every agent onboard, then hurried after him into the hallway, gun clutched in my hand.

Chapter 40

SHE HAMMERED her hand into the door until it became painful. Elena could barely breathe properly when Travis opened it. He looked surprised.

"Did you already do it?"

She walked past him and came inside his room without a word. She went straight to the bed, where she stopped. She was catching her breath, trying to remain as calm as possible.

"What is this?" she asked and showed him the open letter.

The expression on his face changed drastically. His eyes grew wide, and the sides of his mouth turned down.

"You opened it?"

He stepped forward and grabbed the letter out of her hand.

"Travis, what the heck is this?" she said, her voice high-pitched as panic rushed through her body. "What have you done?"

"You weren't supposed to open it," he said, looking up at her.

"That's so not the point here."

"Yes, it is. Don't you see?" he groaned loudly and placed both hands on his head. "Now, you're an accomplice!"

"I would be an accomplice the moment I handed in the letter," she said. "Heck, I already am for helping you, even for bringing you on board, telling them you're my husband so that you can stay here for free. How do you think all of that looks?"

He threw out his arms and grunted, annoyed. "You were just supposed to hand it over to the mother; it was the easiest job in the entire world, and now... look at what you've done. You've ruined everything."

"*I* have ruined everything; oh, will you please...."

"Why?" he asked. "Why on earth would you read it when I specifically asked you not to?"

"I think I'm entitled to know what I'm handing over. I wanted to know what I was getting myself into, and this...," she said with a deep exhale, trying to remain calm. But it was hard. This was worse than when he got arrested for shoplifting, and she had to talk the police officer out of taking him in, or the time those guys were after him because of his gambling debt, and she had to take out a loan to pay them off. This time, he had taken it too far. There were no excuses anymore. He had taken it way too far.

"Travis, this is over the line for me. I don't want any part in it. This is criminal. We could get arrested."

He gave her a strange look. "What did you think it was?"

"I don't know. How was I supposed to know?"

"You must have had some idea at least when I handed you the note?" he said, sounding annoyed. "I mean, here I am offering you a ton of money. How could you think it isn't criminal?"

She paused. "I guess I thought maybe you had some information that you wanted them to pay for—that you had seen something and wanted to tell them but didn't want the police involved, and instead, you wanted to get some money out of it. Maybe I had a feeling it wasn't exactly legal but... not this. I hadn't imagined this. Travis. I can't. I refuse to be a part of it. This is a child."

"You don't mean that," he said, his voice softening so he wouldn't scare her away. He needed her help with this. Anger wasn't the way to approach it. "Come on, Elena. This could be a lot of money."

She glanced toward the bed, where the small feet were sticking out from under the covers, then sighed.

"You're insane, Travis. To think that this would work...."

He grabbed her by the shoulders and forced her to look into his face. "But it will work, Elena. That's the beauty of it. It's gonna work perfectly."

She shook her head with a scoff and pushed him away. "No, it won't. It will fail, and you and I will go to jail."

"No, we won't. We'll be rich. The family will get their child back, and everyone will be happy."

She sighed and rubbed her forehead, then looked at her brother. "Travis. You kidnapped a child. The ship is crawling with FBI and police all looking for this exact child. There's nowhere to run. You have lost touch with reality. They just found the sister to this child at the ice rink. I heard it from some of my coworkers. She was murdered. They will think you killed her." She paused and looked at him again, then at the sleeping girl in the bed.

Her heart was suddenly racing in her chest.

"Did you?"

"Did I what?"

"Did you kill the sister, Travis?" she asked, a sudden panic rushing through her body, spiking the adrenaline. She clasped her mouth when saying the next question.

"Did you... murder that little girl?"

He shook his head violently. "Elena. How could you say such a thing? You know me. I'm your brother."

"Do I, Travis? Do I really know you? Because right now, it feels like I don't. I don't recognize you at all anymore."

"Elena, you must listen to me. I didn't hurt anyone."

"Why do you have the sister, then? I don't understand any of this, Travis. I can't... I'm freaking out here."

He reached out his hands to try and calm her down. "Listen, Elena. I… I didn't kill anyone."

She looked into his eyes, then shook her head. "I don't believe you. I don't know who or what to believe right now, but I know one thing. I can't be a part of this, Travis."

She lifted both hands in the air, pushed back her tears, then walked to the door. "I have covered for you and made excuses for you our entire lives. It ends here. No more."

Then she opened the door and slammed it shut behind her before rushing out into the hallway without hearing the yelling and screaming voices coming up behind her from further down the hallway. When she realized what was happening, it was too late, and someone had grabbed her from behind. A big hairy hand was covering her mouth, a knife was pressed against her throat, and a whispering voice in her ear said, "Say one word, and you're dead."

Chapter 41

"HOLD IT RIGHT THERE."

I had finally caught up to Gerard Hutcheon, who was running down the hallway. I slowed down and pointed my gun at him, then lowered it slowly as I approached him and realized he wasn't alone. A small woman was in his grip, her pleading eyes looking up at me for help. When I saw the knife at her throat, I lowered the gun completely so I wouldn't escalate the situation. Gerard Hutcheon was sweating heavily, his face turning red with the effort from running.

"One step closer, and I kill her," he said.

"Okay, okay," I said and stopped completely. "I just want to talk to you, Gerard. No one has to get hurt."

"Back off," he hissed. "Let me leave the ship"

"Well, I can't really do that," I said. "You hurt my colleague and she is still recovering back in the room from what you did to her."

"I will kill this girl," he said. "Let me go."

"I can't do that," I said.

The woman whimpered as he tightened his grip and pressed the knife into her skin.

"I'm not an idiot," he spat. "Use your radio. Tell someone to make it happen."

"Listen, Gerard," I said. "There is no way this is going to end well for you. We're on a ship. There is nowhere to hide or go. In a few seconds, this hallway will be crawling with FBI agents. You might as well hand me the knife before you do something that you will regret."

He stared at me, contemplating what to do next. I knew that look. He hadn't given up yet.

"Give me a boat," he said. "I don't care about the phone. Just give me a speedboat, so I can get out of here."

I exhaled. "Gerard… they will catch you. We have boats in the water all around the ship. Local Bahamian police will sniff you out faster than you can hide. Just talk to me, will you? We can avoid this ending badly for you, but you need to help me. Tell me what you did to the children. Cooperate, and we are actually very reasonable people. We can figure this out. It doesn't have to end with more people getting hurt, including yourself."

He was breathing heavily, pressing the knife closer to her skin. The woman was hyperventilating now, her eyes in complete panic. I was worried about her and could feel my heart rate go up as she whimpered in fear.

"Just get me the boat, or I will slit her throat. Do you hear me?"

I nodded. "Okay. Okay. If that's how you want to do it. But you're making a choice here. You're the one putting yourself in danger."

"Just get me the boat!"

He was yelling now, and that scared the woman even more. I put my hand out, grabbed my radio, and pressed the button. I stared at the knife on the woman's throat, then at the angry face close behind her. While pretending to be focused on the radio, pressing it with one hand, I swiftly lifted my gun in the other, moving faster than he could react.

Then, I fired a shot. A second later, the bullet ripped through Gerard's shoulder. He dropped the knife in his hand and fell to the ground, limp as a ragdoll.

Part IV

SUNDAY 4 P.M.

Chapter 42

TRAVIS DIDN'T DARE to move. He was on the floor by the bed, where he had been sitting since he heard the shot. He was shaking heavily, his heart beating fast in his chest.

What happened?

He hadn't dared to get up or to look out the peephole. Hearing the shot had scared him so much that he had jumped for cover and been paralyzed, unable to move while listening to the voices on the other side of the door. Right after the shot was fired, everything had gone quiet—eerily quiet. He still hadn't dared to get up and look. He was so certain they were coming for him—that this was it. His time had come. It had to have been his sister who had told them where the girl was.

The silence was soon replaced by a lot of commotion. He heard loud voices talking and footsteps—some were even running, spiking his fear. The activity had been going on for a long time, and he was terrified they would burst down the door any second. So, he hid on the floor behind the bed, bracing himself for them to knock the door down and storm inside, yelling and screaming for him to put his hands in the air.

But so far, they hadn't.

What's taking them so long?

He had wondered if he might be able to escape somehow, but his stateroom didn't even have a window. The only way out was the same way as in.

He lifted his head and stared at the door, then at the girl in his bed. She was blinking her eyes now and making some noises.

She's waking up!

"Mommy?"

Travis jumped up on the bed and grabbed her. Seeing this, the girl immediately started to scream. Fearing they would hear her on the other side of the door, Travis put his hand over her mouth and shushed her while frantically making sure no one could hear her.

The girl was crying behind his hand.

"No, no, it's okay," he whispered. "Don't cry, little girl. I just need you to be very quiet right now. Everything is going to be all right."

The girl's eyes rested on him. She was still sobbing but became quieter, and he nodded reassuringly.

"Can you be quiet for me? I will get you more chicken nuggets or, even better—ice cream. How about that, huh?"

That made the tears stop. The girl stared at him, then nodded.

He smiled, trying to make her feel less afraid of him. If she trusted him, she wouldn't scream.

"Okay," he said, panting. "I'll let go of you now, but you must promise me not to scream again, okay?"

She nodded.

He let go of her and waited a heartbeat, then pulled away from her as she laid back down, quiet.

Then he walked to the door and finally peeked outside in the hallway through the peephole. It was the police who were out there, all right. But they weren't there for him. They were lifting a body onto a stretcher, and he just managed to see the face before it disappeared. Then he saw his sister being taken away by the woman he recognized as the female FBI agent in charge of the investigation.

His heart skipped a beat.

Why had they taken her in? What was she going to tell them?

Was she going to rat him out?

Chapter 43

I WAS STILL SHAKING but trying to hide it. I stared at the body of Gerard Hutcheon as it disappeared on the stretcher and was taken to the ship's infirmary below deck. I had shot him in the shoulder, so he would live, but he was still unconscious.

Elena, the woman who had been held captive, clung to my arm. I knew I had taken a huge risk by shooting him, and I would have to go through an investigation into it, but at that moment, I felt it was the only solution to saving the girl. She was bleeding from where the knife had cut her throat, and I did not doubt that he would have hurt her had I not shot him.

Elena was crying heavily now, and I decided to help her get away from there. Paramedics had cleaned and bandaged the wound on her throat, but she was in a state of deep shock and shouldn't be left alone.

I took her to the security operating room and sat her in a chair. Dana brought a blanket and put it around her.

"Are you okay?" Dana asked, putting a hand on my shoulder.

"Ask me again a little later," I said. "How about you?"

"Oh, I'm fine. It was nothing. Just a bent rib or two. Nothing I can't handle or haven't had before." She said it with a wink, then left us alone. I grabbed Elena's hands in mine.

"Are you okay?"

She looked into my eyes, then nodded. "W-who was he?"

I exhaled. "We don't really know much about him yet."

"Why? Why would he... do that?"

"He was trying to get away from us and using you as leverage."

She looked down at her fingers. She had his blood on the shoulder of her white shirt.

"I'm glad you shot him," she said with a sniffle. "I was so scared."

"Yeah, well, I might be very unpopular for doing so," I said with a sigh. "Now that he is unconscious, he can't tell us where he hid the other girl."

Her eyes grew wide. "H-he took those... girls?"

I shrugged, then rubbed my forehead. "We don't know. I shouldn't be telling you this just yet. But yes, we believe he was involved."

She was barely blinking while staring at me. "You're saying you ran after him because you believe he killed that girl?"

I didn't know how to answer that. The fact was, we still had no idea. All I knew was that this guy hurt my colleague and ran, then kidnapped a woman and held her hostage. I worried that I was going to get in trouble for shooting him.

Dana came up to me. "Can I borrow you for a second?"

I looked at Elena. She was drinking bottled water that I had given her.

"I'll be okay," she said.

I walked outside to meet Dana in the hallway. "We searched his phone really quickly and found these."

She opened the photo app and scrolled through his pictures. I couldn't believe what I was seeing.

"All this was on his phone?"

Dana nodded. "Yup. More than five hundred pictures."

"All of the McCarthy family?"

She nodded. "Yup. And a lot of them of the wife and children. He was definitely obsessed with them. I think he just might be our guy."

She placed a hand on my arm. "I think we got him. No, let me rephrase that. I think *you* got him."

I breathed, relieved, even though my stomach still felt stirred up in a strange knot. I chalked it up to the uneasiness of the situation.

"The only question we need an answer for now is, where is the second girl?" I said. "What did he do with her body?"

Chapter 44

THEN:

He was being more and more careful about what he said. It wasn't that she got mad at him; it was more the way that everything he said became a political issue. And he simply couldn't stand discussing everything all the time. When he came home, he wanted to relax. But Tina was home all the time, so as soon as he stepped inside the door, she wanted to show him what she had seen or tell him about what she had read, and her views became more and more different from his to the point where he simply didn't want to talk anymore.

And then the lying began.

He took the kids to the doctor and had them vaccinated, even though he knew it was against her will. It was a matter of their health, he argued to himself when he felt guilty.

The homeschooling was fine with him as long as it wasn't too much for Tina. He had loved going to school himself and hanging out with his friends, but if she felt so strongly about not letting them go, then that was okay with him. He would meet her on that. But he was worried about what she was teaching them when he wasn't there. She spent night after night still immersed in the videos she watched online, going through one after the other endlessly.

One morning, he came down for breakfast, and she was sitting in the recliner in the living room, rocking back and forth, holding her knees up under her chin. The kids were playing on the floor, building brick towers that kept falling.

"What's the matter? Are you not feeling well?"

Her eyes were bloodshot red. She had been crying.

"Are you sick? Tina? Do you need me to call your mother and have her come over and look after the children? Tina?"

He grabbed her by the shoulder, and she looked up at him. There were tears in her eyes.

"What's wrong?"

"The children," she said.

He stared at their two daughters, Nicky and Becky, who were still playing together. Nine years and two years old—they loved one another and always stuck together. He was so happy that they would always have one another like he and his brother had each other growing up and still did to this day.

"The children are fine, Tina. Look, they're playing together. There's nothing to worry about."

"No," she said with a sniffle. "Not our children."

He gave her a strange look. "Then what children are we talking about?"

"All the children. Don't you know that there are pedophile rings trafficking children?"

He exhaled. "Yes, I know. And that is awful, of course, but…."

"You do know that it's the politicians who traffic them, right? Along with the so-called elite. The rich. The Illuminati will kidnap, torture, and eat little children in military bases underground. And they're all reptiles."

"They… what?"

"Pizza gate. Have you not heard about that?"

"What?"

"You must keep up, Bryan. Pay attention to the world around you. The world is ruled by the lizards, Bryan, don't you see? Look at them," she said and showed him a picture of a famous politician on her phone. "The teeth, Bryan. Look for the lizard teeth. They all have them. She does, and this...." She flipped to another picture of another famous and influential politician. "Look at this guy's teeth, Bryan, and the eyes. Don't tell me those are human eyes. They're reptiles, I tell you—all of them. And they're coming for our children. Our children can never leave the house. Do you hear me? They must stay inside always, so these monsters won't get to them."

Chapter 45

"I'VE ASKED you both to be here because we believe we might have had a breakthrough in your case. I have put you together, believing you can act civilly toward one another, am I right?"

I stared at Tina, then at Bryan McCarthy. They nodded after a few seconds of thinking. The three of us were sitting in the captain's quarters on his white leather couches. I had faith that they would be able to talk without getting into a fight since the blame was now pointing at someone from the outside. Plus, I simply didn't have the time to sit down with each of them and have the same conversation twice. Time was running out for me. The pressure to let people leave the ship was building. Captain Larsen had informed me that, so far, they had to stop three fights in bars and on the pool deck, and four people were now in the ship's detention, sleeping it off.

"Have you found Becky?" Bryan asked, his voice trembling.

"Not yet," I said. "But we're searching our suspect's room and belongings right now in the hope that we might find something that can lead us to her whereabouts. Hopefully, we will find her soon."

Tina's eyes grew wide. "Alive?"

I exhaled. "I think you might need to prepare yourself for the worst-case scenario here."

"You don't think she's alive anymore?" Bryan asked.

I hesitated. This was a hard one. "Personally, I always tend to keep up hope until I see a body, but I have to admit that it doesn't look good. With what we now know happened to her sister, and how long Becky has been gone with no proof of life…." I paused for a beat when seeing their faces grow pale.

"I'm sorry."

Tina shook her head. "No, no, you're just being honest."

"Who is he?" Bryan asked. "The guy who took our children?"

"His name is Gerard Hutcheon," I said.

I pulled up a photo of him from my phone and showed it to them. "We're trying to establish his connection to your family. So, please, if you will, look at the picture here. Have you seen this man before?"

I handed the phone to Tina, who took the first glance. She stared at the screen, her fingers on her other hand tapping on her thigh.

"Do you recognize him?" I asked.

She stared at it for a little while longer. "I want to say yes, but he looks, well, quite ordinary. I think I might have seen him here on the ship, yes. Now, I remember. I saw him up on the pool deck on the day that the children disappeared. He was sitting in one of the lounge chairs."

"Let me see," Bryan said and grabbed the phone out of her hand. He stared at the picture, then shook his head. "Doesn't look familiar to me at all."

"Try to look again," I urged. "If your wife says she has seen him, then chances are you have too."

He looked again, then shook his head. "Nope. Never seen him in my life."

He handed me back the phone.

"I did tell Bryan I believed we were being followed—that someone was watching us," Tina said.

"Oh, here we go again," he said, leaning back on the couch.

"But you wouldn't believe me," she continued unabated. "He never believes me when I say stuff like that. Because I'm just the crazy one, right? Well, see where that got us?"

"So, now it's my fault?" Bryan said.

"You never want to believe me," she said, raising her voice. "It doesn't matter what I say. I'm just crazy."

He scoffed loudly.

"See, there you go again," she continued, annoyed.

I put a hand on her arm to get her to focus on me. "I need you to look at the photo again," I said and handed the phone back to her. "And tell me if this was the man who threw you overboard."

"I told you I didn't see his face."

"But maybe there's something else you recognize? Like his hands? He's got a skull tattoo on his wrist; maybe you have seen that? If you swipe sideways, there's a close-up photo of the tattoo."

She swiped, then looked at the photo. "I have never seen that tattoo before. I would definitely have remembered that. I would have noticed that big of a tattoo."

"And he wasn't wearing gloves?" I asked.

"I don't think so. To be honest, I don't remember it much, only that I couldn't breathe and then passed out," she said determinedly. "I told you; I already know who it was, but you still won't believe me. You can tell me that this guy hurt my children and pushed me in the water all that you want to, but I know the truth."

She sent her husband a look, and he grunted.

"May I ask why you think this man took our children? What is it based upon?" Bryan asked.

I nodded. "Of course. We found photos on his phone. More than five hundred of them of you and your family and lots of them were of the children playing in the pool area. He has a prior of having tried to buy someone's child—twice."

"It was a sexual thing?" Bryan asked, wrinkling his nose at the thought. "I can't believe it."

"We don't know the motive for him taking your children yet, but it might have been."

"Oh, dear God," Bryan said and hid his face between his hands. "This is just getting worse and worse."

Tina stared at him, shaking her head. Then, she paused. "But how? How could he even get into the room? To *our* room? Don't you think I would have noticed if some stranger had come into our room? I don't buy it. Bryan did this to me, to us. I just know it."

"We still don't know how he was able to get into your room," I said. "Right now, our focus is mainly on locating Becky."

Tina whimpered. "You mean her dead body, don't you? You believe she is dead?"

I went quiet, not knowing what to tell them. I tried hard not to think of myself and my own children and if it had been one of them missing on this ship and me waiting for their dead body to show up.

The thought was unbearable.

"You did it; don't think I don't know it," Tina suddenly said, addressed to Bryan.

"Do you see how she is twisting everything constantly?" he said, addressed to me. "Always finding a way to blame me. For everything."

He looked at Tina and threw out his arms. "The police and the freaking FBI even believe this guy hurt you and the children. And you think you know better? You're insane, woman. Are you even listening to them? Are you hearing anything being said, or are you just making your own crazy conclusions as usual?"

"You could have paid this man to do it for all I know," she said. "Maybe that's why you wanted to go on this stupid cruise. It gave you an alibi. I told you there were pedophiles onboard these things stealing children to eat them or do God knows what to them. I told you this would happen. I told you! I just never thought it would be you." She got to her feet, ran for the door, and pulled it open while yelling.

"Get me out of here. I can't stand being in the same room as him anymore."

Chapter 46

TRAVIS SHUT the door to the room behind him, then hurried into the carpeted hallway. He got in an elevator and looked out the big windows as he soared upward, staring at the people walking the marble tiles in the mall area below and watching as they grew smaller. On the top floor, he got out.

Just as he stepped outside, someone rushed past him and almost ran into him as they hurried into the elevator he had just left. It took him a second to realize who she was. It wasn't until the doors closed, and they locked eyes for just a brief moment, that he knew.

It was her.

The mom.

Travis pressed the button to the elevator again, then turned to see if another was open. It took a few seconds before he heard the *ding* sound as the elevator next to him opened up. He got in, then looked down through the glass and saw that the mom had gotten out in the mall area.

He pressed the button and followed her.

Seconds later, he was down there, surrounded by the many shops, bars, and restaurants on each side like pearls on a string.

There was everything your heart could desire: souvenirs, clothing, chocolate, ice cream, coffee, newly baked pastries, and, of course, alcohol.

A man walked past him holding a big yellow plastic cup with a straw sticking out. Not once did he cease sipping from it as he zigzagged down the halls, swaying from side to side. Travis avoided bumping into him—yet only barely—by walking around him, then he bumped into a young woman wearing a shirt saying, *I'll bring the booze.* Travis said his excuses, not only to her but also to her boyfriend next to her, who was wearing a similar shirt, stating, *I'll bring the attitude.*

He spotted the mom further ahead as she approached a crowd of people who had stopped to watch the dancing crew members wearing eighties neon costumes and wigs while playing Madonna from a boombox.

Everyone onboard was holding the same colorful refillable plastic cups of alcohol, which they sipped on from a straw. Some were yelling at the dancers, others at their own families. The noise level was high, and Travis elbowed his way through while it was announced over the speakers that it was time for the belly flop competition at the pool deck upstairs.

"Excuse me," he said and tried to push past a couple who didn't move one inch but kept sipping their straws and blocking his way. He went behind them instead and almost stepped on a little kid with an ice cream in his hand, wearing swim trunks with tiny sharks on them. He smiled at him when he spotted the mom by the candy store and hurried after her, pushing through the people. The crowd became smaller, and he could soon move freely again as four big guys came out from a bar and started to punch one another while yelling loudly.

If it was fun or serious, Travis couldn't tell, but he hurried past them and spotted the mom again as she slowed down, getting nearer the entrance to the casino. She walked inside, sat at the bar, and ordered a Gin and Tonic.

"This one is on me," Travis told the bartender, then sat on the stool next to her. She turned her head and smiled.

"Thanks, I needed it."

"So… you're that mom, aren't you?" he asked as their drinks arrived.

"I am a mom, yes," she said and drank.

"You know what I mean," he said.

She scoffed. "Yeah. Here I thought I could sneak down and get a drink without anyone noticing."

"It's okay," he said. "Your secret is safe with me. I think everyone else here is too drunk to recognize you or even care."

She downed her entire drink, then put the glass down.

"Another one?" he asked.

She exhaled, then nodded. "Yes, please."

He stood up and signaled the waiter. While he did, he snuck the letter into her jacket pocket without her seeing it.

Chapter 47

"ARE you just gonna let her leave?"

Bryan glared down at me. He stood up, reaching his hand toward the door where Tina had just disappeared. "Technically, she is still a suspect, right?"

"Let her go," I said. "She needs to cool down. We're on a ship."

He pointed an angry finger at me. "I'm telling you, she's very clever, that one. Don't let her get away with this."

"So far, no one is going anywhere," I said, feeling a little tired of listening to those two. "No one is leaving the ship."

He sat down on the couch and shook his head. "She's hiding something. I just know she is. I know that look in her eyes."

I stared at him, wondering how two people who were supposed to love one another could suddenly be so vicious to each other. Then I remembered my own marriage to Chad and how it had grown sour over the years until he cheated on me. I realized that I wasn't one to talk.

"I bet you she hired this guy, that... Hutcheon guy to murder the children, and then she jumped overboard by herself to make it look like she was attacked. It would totally be something she would do."

"But why?" I asked. "Why would she kill her own children?"

He wrinkled his forehead and leaned forward, folding his hands in his lap. "Because she is nuts."

I tilted my head. "That's not really a motive, is it?"

"She had this idea… that… that…." he paused.

"That what?"

He leaned back again. "You're not gonna believe me anyway."

I wanted to tell him to "try me," but we were interrupted by a loud knock on the door. Dana peeked in.

"We have a situation."

I got up and followed her into the hallway.

"What's going on?"

"It's that girl, the one you saved when Hutcheon took her hostage?"

"Yes?"

"She doesn't seem completely well."

"How so?"

"She's talking gibberish and making absolutely no sense. I don't really know what to do with her."

I sighed. "She's probably in a state of deep shock. What does the doctor say who attended to her?"

"That she is physically fine. But I tried to talk to her to find out where she was staying and help her get back to her room, but she kept jabbering about her brother and the casino and something about small feet under the covers. I… I don't know what to do with her."

"She's part of the cleaning crew, right?"

Dana nodded. "Yes. I spoke to one of her colleagues, and she says that, apparently, her husband is onboard."

"Do you know which room?" I asked.

"I wrote it down," she said, then handed me a note.

I looked at it. "I'll go and talk to him."

Chapter 48

THEN:

"It seems that every time I leave for a game and come back, it's gotten worse."

Bryan looked at his brother across the living room. Darryl's wife, Bette, walked in and sat down, handing them each a beer.

"Two days ago, when I returned, she had changed all our phone numbers again. She even took my phone and stepped on it, saying, 'You never know who is listening.' Then she handed me a new one she had bought with a new number. This is the third time this year we're changing phones and numbers. It's driving me crazy. My friends don't know how to reach me, and I lose all their numbers every time."

Bette nodded compassionately. She was drinking white wine. "Have you tried to get her to see someone professional?"

"You mean like a shrink?" he asked. "Yes, I have suggested it several times, but she gets angry with me and tells me that I just want her locked up because I think she's crazy."

"She should be locked up," Darryl said with a scoff. "But that's just my honest opinion."

Bette gave him a look. "Darryl, that's not very nice."

He shrugged. "Maybe not, but I always thought something was wrong with that woman."

Bette got up, then went and sat next to Bryan on the couch. She put her hand on his arm. "I'm so sorry, Bryan. But you have to try and get her to see someone. Maybe even a relationship counselor?"

"Couples therapy?" Darryl said. "There's nothing wrong with *him*. She's the one who needs help."

Bette looked at him again. "I think Bryan needs help too. They both need advice on how to deal with all this. Tina is getting increasingly paranoid, and it's hard on both of them."

"I still say he should have her locked up and throw away the key," Darryl said, drinking from his beer. "But I guess that's just me."

"Don't listen to him," Bette said. "You have to think about the children."

"The children are exactly who I am thinking about," Darryl said. "They shouldn't be around someone like that—giving them crazy ideas. She's even homeschooling them. Who knows what she's telling them when you aren't there."

"I just... I don't know how to deal with this anymore. She's a firm believer that movie stars are pedophiles, and I can't even watch the news at night without her getting angry with me and saying that I'm a sheep and that I should watch some truths instead, and then she shows me these videos online, and it blows my mind."

"Do you still love her?"

He nodded. "I do, I really, really do."

"Then you need to put down an ultimatum," Darryl said. "Tell her to see a professional, or you want to separate."

He stared at him. "I... I can't do that."

"Why not?" Darryl said.

Bryan looked down. "Because... what if she says she wants to get a divorce?"

"Then you get the heck out of there," Darryl said. "And count yourself lucky that you got out of this marriage in time."

Bette sighed. "Darryl isn't completely wrong, tactless but not wrong. Telling Tina to see a professional isn't a bad idea. You need to do something. You can't keep living like this."

Chapter 49

HE BROUGHT a pizza slice back to the girl, watched her eat it, and then handed her the ice cream he had promised her. She didn't say a word but dug in and ate greedily. Travis breathed calmly, thinking of the letter, wondering if the mom had found it yet. He kept imagining her sticking her hand inside that hooded jacket she was wearing with her jean shorts and pulling it out. She had to have done it by now.

Right?

He shook his head.

Of course, she did.

He looked at his watch; he still had time. The girl slurped her soda and seemed to be feeling more comfortable. He was hoping she would fall back asleep. He had crushed a couple of Ambien and put them into the soda. That should keep her down for another couple of hours, at least.

Then, he could do his business.

"Are you feeling better?" he asked and took the empty pizza box and ice cream container. He threw both in the trash can.

She nodded.

"Feeling sleepy?" he asked.

She nodded again and rubbed her eyes. He smiled, satisfied with his own cleverness.

"Can I watch TV?" she asked.

"Sure," he said and turned it on. He found Cartoon Network, and she seemed happy about whatever show they were playing.

"Lay down if you feel tired," he said.

She did and closed her eyes halfway, then opened them again. Then, she started to cry.

"Oh, no, why are you crying, little girl?"

He felt helpless. He really couldn't have her making this kind of noise. Someone could walk by outside and hear her. It might cause suspicion.

"It's okay, little girl," he said, patting her hair clumsily. "Everything is going to be just fine."

"Nicky," she mumbled between sobs. "Nicky."

And then, she burst into heavier cries, and Travis had no idea what to do. He just prayed that the sleeping pills would kick in soon.

"Shh, shh, it's gonna be okay."

"Mommy," she said.

"It's okay," he said and patted her hair again. "It's gonna be okay."

She calmed down slightly, and so did he, while Gumball and Darwin were grinning on the TV screen. He looked at the clock again; there was still plenty of time. He was in no hurry. He just hoped she would find the letter in time. And he prayed that Elena wasn't selling him out to the police right now.

It was going to be okay. He had said it to calm the girl, and now he was saying it to calm himself down.

That's when he heard the knock on the door, and everything inside of him stopped as he heard the voice coming from behind it, "Hello? Mr. Gasgarth? It's the FBI. Please, open the door."

Chapter 50

"HELLO?"

I knocked again on the heavy door.

"Mr. Gasgarth?"

I knocked again—still, no answer.

"This is Agent Thomas; I'm with the FBI. I need to talk to you, Mr. Gasgarth. Please, open your door. It's about your wife."

I heard fiddling behind the door, and seconds later, it cracked open. A face appeared, and he smiled in a friendly way before sliding out and closing the door tightly behind him. I couldn't help but think that it was stunning how married people sometimes began to look like one another over the years. He was the spitting image of his wife.

"Mr. Gasgarth?"

He nodded. "Yes?"

"I'm here about your wife, Elena?"

He tilted his head. "What about her? Is she okay?"

"Well, to be honest, I'm not too sure. There was an incident, actually, right here in the hallway. Someone was running from the police, and he tried to take her hostage but was shot. You might have heard it?"

I looked at him, wondering if this was news to him or not. He shook his head. "I haven't been in the room all day. I was… at the casino upstairs."

"Ah, okay, that makes sense," I said.

He swallowed. "What happened to Elena? Where is she now?"

"You should probably come to see her since she is in a state of shock, and we can't really make sense of what she is saying."

His eyes lit up, and he bit his lip. "Oh, really? She hasn't told you anything? I mean, anything important for your investigation?"

I wrinkled my forehead and stared at the man in front of me, puzzled. I shook the feeling and told him to follow me. We walked down the hallway, then took the secret passageways to the elevator used only by the cruise personnel. I was learning my way around this ship quickly and knew the best ways to avoid the public.

We got into the elevator and went up to the security room, where Elena sat with Dana. She rose to her feet when I entered.

"Thank God."

"This is Mrs. Gasgarth's husband," I said and pointed at the man behind me.

"Oh, what a relief," Dana said. "She is making no sense."

Mr. Gasgarth stepped forward and grabbed his wife's hand in his. "Elena? Dear? It's Travis. Are you okay?"

Elena stared at him, then started to cry. "Oh, Travis. It was horrible. I don't know what to do."

He pulled her into a hug for comfort. I felt relieved yet oddly uneasy in his presence. There was something about this guy that rubbed me the wrong way. I just couldn't quite put a finger on it. He seemed like he was hiding something. But then again, a lot of people acted strangely when the police came around, especially the FBI. Most people hid things and felt guilty around us. It was normal.

"She's in shock, the poor thing," he said, still hugging her. "Shh, it will be okay, Elena. Come, let's go back to the room."

Elena nodded, crying heavily. "Oh, no, Travis. I can't do that—I can't do it anymore. We have to tell them. Please, tell them."

Travis shook his head and chuckled nervously. "She doesn't know what she's saying. I'll take her back to the room, and maybe a nap will help her calm down."

He helped her get up from the chair and put her arm around his shoulder. "There you go. Let's get you into bed."

He helped her toward the door when Elena suddenly stopped. "The little feet, Travis. The little feet under the covers."

He shook his head. "You've been through a lot today. You're making no sense, sweetie. Come, let's get you back to the room. I'm sorry that she couldn't be of more help."

He said the last addressed to Dana and me, and I watched him help Elena out the door while something was stirring inside me. All the red flags were showing up, but I just didn't know why.

At least not yet.

Chapter 51

THEN:

He slept at his brother's and didn't come home until the next day. All the way back in his car, he rehearsed what to say to Tina once he walked through the door.

"We need to talk... this can't go on. You need to see someone... a professional... a therapist or this marriage is over."

He mumbled the words to himself in the cabin of his new Mercedes while the rain hammered down on his window. The weather had been bad for a few days in their area, and he was getting tired of it. So much rain had fallen that his pool had flooded. He noticed it as he parked the car in the driveway after driving through the gate to their house.

"I fear that you are having a psychotic breakdown," he said as he stopped the engine of the car and the garage door closed behind him. Then he shook his head. "No, that's taking it too far. She won't react well to that. Keep it simple."

He got out of the car inside the garage and slammed the door shut.

"See a therapist, or this marriage is over."

He grabbed the door leading to the kitchen and pulled it open, thinking, *yes, that's what I'm going to say. Plain and simple.*

He took a deep breath to steady himself as he walked inside and called out. "I'm home."

Nicky was the first to run toward him and hug his legs.

"Daddy-y-y-y."

Becky came out later and stood for a few seconds in the doorway, looking at him.

"Hi, sweetie. Are you okay?"

"What's wrong with Mommy?" she asked.

He put Nicky down, and she took off, staggering toward her toys. "What do you mean? Is something wrong?"

Becky looked down, then back up at her father. He saw it in her eyes. Something was very wrong, and it scared him.

"Where is she?" he asked.

"In the basement."

He nodded and put a hand on Becky's shoulder. "I'll take care of it. Don't worry, okay?"

"It's kind of hard not to," she mumbled.

He walked to the stairs and took a couple of steps down.

"Tina? You down here?"

No answer. But the lights were on, so he kept going. "Tina? Honey? Are you in the basement?"

"In here," he heard her voice say, and he walked into the room in the back, one that they usually used for storage.

"What are you doing?" he asked and stepped inside, then paused. He couldn't believe what he was seeing. She had turned the room into a bunker with bunkbeds and more canned goods than they could eat in months.

"W-what's going on here?"

Tina looked up. She was holding something between her hands. When Bryan saw what it was, he let out a light gasp and took a step back.

"What on earth are you doing with that?"

Chapter 52

"THAT WAS ODD, don't you think?"

Dana had gotten me a cup of coffee from the café downstairs and handed it to me. She looked at me with her big brown eyes. She sipped her coffee before she asked, "What?"

I sipped mine as well and shook my head. "Those two. What she said."

Dana shrugged. "She was in shock. It made no sense what she said. Can you blame her for losing it after what she went through? What you did, shooting the guy was pretty risky. She could have been hit."

"I knew what I was doing. I never miss a shot."

The coffee was too hot to drink, but I did it anyway and burned my tongue. I was hoping it would make me feel more awake. I was getting tired—it had been a long day.

"But that part about the little feet," I said. "The little feet under the covers. I can't stop thinking about it."

"Do you think she was talking about Becky?" Dana asked.

"It just doesn't make much sense, does it?" I said and grabbed a cookie from the packet Dana had brought back with the coffee. The chocolate chip cookie was giant, almost as big as my hand, and so soft it melted on my tongue. Just what I needed. A shot of sugar and caffeine to keep me going.

"I mean, I saw Gerard Hutcheon grab her and put a knife to her throat. If he kidnapped the children and killed them, how would Elena and her husband fit into that scenario?"

"They don't. She was just a cleaning lady in the wrong place at the wrong time," Dana said and grabbed a cookie as well. She bit into it, and some chocolate got stuck on her upper lip.

"Yeah, I'm sure you're right," I said and ate more, then washed it down with the coffee. My fingers were tapping on the side of the paper cup while my mind raced to put the pieces together. I knew I had to let it go, but my instinct kept telling me I was onto something.

"I mean, we know that Gerard Hutcheon was obsessed with the McCarthy family and the children," Dana said. "There's nothing that indicates that he was working with anyone else. He was one sick man operating on his own, right?"

I nodded. "Maybe, yes."

"But I sense you don't believe that," Dana said.

"It's just…." I paused and sighed. "What do we know about Elena and Travis Gasgarth?" I sat up straight. "Wait. Wasn't her name in the file of background checks that had priors?"

I grabbed the phone and opened the file again. "Yes, here she is. Elena Maria Gasgarth. And will you look at this?"

"What?"

I showed her my phone.

"She has a prior for kidnapping a minor."

Dana's eyes grew wide. "What?"

"Fifteen years ago."

Dana stared at me. "But she couldn't have been much more than a teenager herself?"

I nodded. "Eighteen. And look who she kidnapped?"

Dana glared at my phone again and scrolled the document. Her eyes met mine. "This makes no sense?"

I nodded, taking back the phone.

"Exactly. I think we need to have another chat with her."

Chapter 53

TRAVIS OPENED the door to his room and helped Elena inside. He slammed it shut behind him with a deep exhale.

"Go sit down," he said. "I'll bring you some water."

He walked to the mini fridge and pulled out a bottle of water, then handed it to Elena, who had sat down on the couch. She smiled and took it, then looked in the direction of the bed. Her shoulders came down.

"Oh. You weren't lying."

"What's that?"

"The girl," she said. "You were right when you said she isn't here anymore. Did you get her back with her mom?"

Travis almost choked on his water. He stared at the bed, unable to believe what he was seeing.

"What in the...?"

He walked to the bed, then pulled off the covers. "Pillows," he mumbled angrily. "Nothing but pillows underneath it."

He then walked to the bathroom and pulled the door open. She wasn't in there either. He shook his head.

"No, no, no, no."

"What's wrong?" Elena asked.

"She has to be here somewhere," he said, then hurried back to the bed and checked behind it.

But she wasn't there either.

Could she be hiding somewhere?

He went down onto his knees and looked under the bed. There was a compartment there meant to store suitcases. He pulled it out in the hope that she was hiding in it.

But no.

Sweat sprang to his forehead. He felt his hands get clammy. "This can't be happening."

"What?" Elena asked. "What can't be happening?"

He was breathing heavily now while spinning around to scan the room for possible hideouts.

"She can't be gone," he said, like Elena would know what he was talking about. "I gave her the pills."

"What pills? What are you talking about, Travis?"

"The sleeping pills. She's supposed to be asleep...."

He paused and looked at the soda he had given her. Then he lifted it and took off the lid. He literally felt the blood leave his face.

"She didn't drink it," he said.

"She... who didn't drink what?"

"The girl," he said, annoyed that he had to explain everything. "She didn't drink her soda. That's why she isn't sleeping."

"So... you didn't give her back to her mom?" Elena asked. He could hear her getting upset now. "I thought you said you took care of it."

Travis stared at the soda in his hand, then at the door in front of him.

Could she have...?

He shook his head. "No. Oh, please, no."

Elena got to her feet. "Travis, what are you doing? You gotta stop this. Please, before you get us into more trouble. The poor girl needs to go back to her mother."

"I have to go find her," he said and put the soda on the table. "I have to find her now."

Elena stood in his way. "Oh, no, you don't. Consider yourself lucky that no one knows she was here. I can clean the room, so there is no trace of her. Hopefully, she will go back to be with her mom, and no one will ever know where she has been."

Elena crossed her arms in front of her chest. "If you go look for her now, I will tell that FBI woman what you did. The only reason I haven't so far is that I might be considered an accomplice. And since I have a prior, I will go away for a very long time."

"I'm going after her," he said. "I want that money."

"No, you don't."

She blocked his way. Their eyes locked, and hers were full of deep determination. She was shaking her head, and he knew that look on his sister's face. He had seen it many times before.

But this time, he didn't care.

"Get out of my way."

She shook her head. "No, Travis. I can't let you do this."

"Move."

She shook her head. "I won't."

"Move out of my way, I said."

"No. I can't let you ruin both of our lives like this."

He tried to push past her, but she pushed him back.

"I don't want to hurt you," he said.

"You won't hurt me."

"Wouldn't I?"

"You wouldn't dare. I'm your sister, Travis. I'm the only family you've got," she said.

He stared into her eyes, anger rising inside of him. He loved his sister dearly; he really did.

But right now, she was in his way.

"I'm sorry," he said.

He then grabbed her by the throat and knocked her into the wall behind her. Elena stared down at him in shock until the air was pushed out of her lungs, and her eyes rolled back into her head as she lost consciousness. She became limp between his hands, and he carried her to the couch, where he set her down gently and put a blanket over her small body. Then, he caressed her gently on the cheek.

"I really am sorry, sis," he mumbled while placing a kiss on her forehead. "But I had to do it. I hope you'll forgive me one day."

Chapter 54

THEN:

Bryan stared at the AK-47 between Tina's hands, then looked up at his wife. His once so sweet and innocent wife who couldn't hurt a spider even when it crawled on her leg—who could never hurt anyone. At least, he never thought she would. But maybe he was wrong. In this second, he was suddenly sure he was very, very wrong.

"Why are you holding an assault rifle?"

"We need to prepare."

"Prepare?"

Tina nodded. "Yes, we need to get ready."

He shook his head slowly, feeling like he had to tread lightly here. The weapon between her hands was a whole new level of crazy—one he had not seen coming—not even a little bit.

"Ready?" he said, wrinkling his forehead. Was this a dream? A joke? "Ready for what?"

She tilted her head slightly. "For the civil war."

He felt how his eyes grew wide in shock. "What... what are you talking about? What civil war?"

"Oh, it's coming," she said. "We need to mobilize. I'm preparing the basement with non-perishables, water, gas, and whatever necessities we'll need to stay alive. Once I'm done, we can live down here for years."

He looked around the room in the basement and all the boxes that hadn't been unpacked.

"But... but why on earth would we live here for years?"

"Because of the war," she said.

"I'm not sure... sweetie, how about you put that thing down.... How... why are you holding a rifle inside our house? With the children right upstairs?"

"We need to start amassing weapons," she said, obviously not sharing his concerns.

She peeked inside the box in front of her, and Bryan did too. He then realized there were more guns inside it. He could barely breathe.

"Where did you get all this stuff?"

"It doesn't matter," she said. "Listen, you need to trust me on this. We don't have time to discuss this."

He shook his head, unable to believe the scene unfolding before his eyes. Was this really his wife? What happened to her?

"Also, we need to start converting our currency into gold and silver," she said unabated. "When the civil war happens, we'll need something to trade with other people."

Oh, my God, she's serious, isn't she? This isn't even a bad joke?

"But... but, sweetie," he said, his heart beating fast in his chest. "Hey, there, how about we go upstairs and talk a little? Maybe you can explain this some more to me because—by God—I'm not sure I fully understand what is going on here. Can we do that? Can we go upstairs and just... talk? Please?"

She paused, then stared at him.

"Have you heard nothing I just told you? There's no time to talk, Bryan. We need action. I'm planning on joining the militia, and I need to prepare. What don't you understand about that?"

Chapter 55

I KNOCKED ON THE DOOR. Dana was beside me and sent me a concerned look when no one opened it.

"Mrs. Gasgarth? Mr. Gasgarth?" I yelled. "This is Agent Thomas with the FBI; can you please open the door?"

Still nothing.

I knocked again, this time harder.

"Elena? Travis? Are you in there?"

Still, nothing happened. I sent Dana a worried glance.

"I don't feel good about this. Something isn't right. I need access to this room," I said. "Call Captain Larsen."

Two minutes later, the captain came rushing down the hallway toward me. He smiled politely.

"I need access to this room," I said. "We believe the second missing child might be in there."

Captain Larsen sighed. He was troubled. "I really don't know if that is... I mean, we have policies, and don't you need, like... a warrant for that?"

I gave him a look of surprise. He had been so cooperative up until now.

"I mean…," he continued. "We are the safest vacation option in the world. And we're darn proud of it. We want to maintain that reputation. We do a lot to make our passengers feel safe and like everything is smooth sailing, so to speak. If I let you into someone's room without their consent, then I'm afraid… what I'm trying to say is that the cruise line is concerned that this whole affair will give us a bad reputation, and they've asked me to minimize the damage. If it comes out that…."

"I will take the blame," I said. "I will talk to your superiors afterward and take any complaints they may have. But this is a child we're talking about. And if you don't open the door for me, I will break it down, which will cost you money to fix, which I am pretty sure will make your superiors even angrier. Not to mention the even worse publicity it will give when the story comes out in the media that you refused to help the police save a child. I think it's in all of our interests that you open the door. Please."

Captain Larsen swallowed. Then he nodded anxiously.

"Yes. Yes, of course."

He signaled his officer next to him to open the door. He tapped the key card on the plate, and it clicked open. I pushed the door while yelling.

"Mr. and Mrs. Gasgarth, we're coming inside. Now."

With my gun pulled, I walked inside first, with Dana right behind me.

"Anyone in here? Lay down on the floor with your hands above your head."

I walked into the bedroom and saw her on the couch. She was tied up with duct tape on her mouth and around her hands and legs.

"Elena," I said, then hurried to her. Dana checked the bathroom and behind the bed while I put my gun away.

"Room's clear," she said.

I knelt next to Elena, then pulled off the tape from her mouth. She was crying. "I'm so, so sorry. I feel awful. Please."

I helped her get her hands loose, then her legs, and she sat up.

"Are you okay?" I asked.

She nodded with a sniffle.

"What happened?" I asked.

She was hyperventilating now, and a few words left her lips between gasps, but I couldn't understand any of them.

"Just breathe," I said. "Take it easy, okay?"

She took a deep breath and calmed down slowly.

"Now, tell me what's going on."

She nodded slowly and looked at her fingers. "Okay. Okay. Oh, God. I am so sorry. I am so, so sorry for... that girl, and... her parents...."

"Breathe again. Try to calm down for me, then explain it all. Now, Travis isn't your husband, is he? He's your brother?"

She nodded. "Yes. We pretended he was my husband so he could come on the ship with me for free. We get three trips for free a year for our spouses."

"And you have the same last name, so that worked well."

"Yes. They never questioned it. I bunk with the other cleaning crew while he is in this room."

"And none of your colleagues asked any questions?"

She shook her head. "Everyone does it."

"I see. Now tell me about the girl. She was here?"

Elena swallowed hard, then nodded. "Oh, God, I feel so awful. When they found her sister in that suitcase...," she paused and sobbed. "He killed her, didn't he?"

"That's what we're trying to find out. We don't know the details yet, but your brother took the children?" I asked.

She sniffled, then looked at me.

"Yes, he took them. And it's all my fault. I gave him my key so he could get into their room last night. He said he just wanted to grab some cash, you know, to play at the casino. Lots of people leave out cash, especially the rich ones, and they don't remember how much they had. It was going to be the last time, he promised me. How was I supposed to know he would... take the children?"

Chapter 56

WAS it suddenly hot on the ship, or was he just sweating because he was anxious? Travis felt the droplets as they tickled his upper lip, then he wiped them away. But as soon as he did, new ones appeared, and more followed on his forehead and in the palms of his clammy hands.

Where would I go if I were a ten-year-old girl?

He went to the deck outside, then walked around it until he couldn't go any further. He then went inside and up and down the mall area, looking into every shop and paying extra attention to the ice cream shops.

But still no sign of her.

Could she have tried to make it back to the room she was in with her family?

Travis hurried back into the elevator and pressed the button to the 8th floor, then hurried out and into the hallway. As he approached the room, he realized she couldn't have gone there. The forensics team was still searching it, and the doorway was blocked by police tape.

He couldn't let them see him there, so he rushed past, nodding at the security officers and FBI agents, pretending he was on his way to a room further down the hallway. Once he was past them, he found an exit and entered the stairwell.

Where could she have gone?

He looked at his watch. It was almost time.

He rushed up the stairs, running as fast as he could until he reached the top deck and entered the pool area.

It was packed with people with nothing else to do. A belly flop competition was taking place in one of the pools, and people had gathered to cheer on the big-bellied men as they dove into the water, making the biggest splash possible.

But no sign of the girl anywhere.

He walked to the kiddy pool area and scanned it, but she wasn't there either. She wasn't by the surfing pool, the climbing wall, or the basketball court.

He sighed and decided to move forward as if nothing had happened. He walked to the bow of the ship and stood by the railing, then looked at his watch.

He was right on time.

Travis kept his cool, and a woman came up next to him seconds later. They didn't look at one another, but he knew who it was.

It was the mom, and she was right on time as well—just like he had told her to be in the letter.

"Are you the guy who claims to have my daughter?"

He nodded. "Yup."

"You got some nerve," she said.

He shrugged. "Guess so."

"And you want money?"

"Yup."

She sighed. "What if I tell you I don't believe you?"

He looked at her. "Excuse me?"

"Do you have any proof that you have her?"

He couldn't believe her. But he had come prepared in case

something like this happened. He pulled out one of the girl's hair ties from his pocket and showed it to her.

"Recognize this?"

She looked at it, then scoffed. "That could have come from any child."

He stared at her. She didn't even bother to look at him but stared out at the ocean. "Listen, lady. I have your daughter. Do you want her back or not?"

Finally, she looked at him. "I don't believe you."

"Then, why did you come?"

"Because I wanted to see what kind of scumbag tries to black-mail a mom who is grieving her missing children. Do you have any idea what I have gone through these past twenty-four hours?"

"Excuse me? Are you even interested in getting your child back?"

"I need more proof," she said. "Get me that, and maybe we will talk."

Travis was about to protest, but before he could, the woman turned her back on him and started to walk away. He stared at her back as it disappeared, unable to fathom what had just happened.

Had the whole darn world lost their minds?

I gotta find that girl if it's the last thing I do!

Chapter 57

"WHEN I WAS EIGHTEEN, I kidnapped my brother from his foster home."

Elena sniffled and wiped her nose. We had been talking for a little, and I was beginning to get a picture of who we were dealing with here.

"That's why I have a prior for kidnapping," she said. "They wouldn't let me have him, so I took him from the home. They were treating him poorly there—like really bad, but there wasn't anything I could do. I wanted to take care of him. I was old enough. But they wouldn't let me, so I got arrested. I'm not a bad person; you must believe me. I didn't know anything about what Travis was up to."

"But you're saying he took the children from the room last night because he wanted to blackmail the parents for money?"

She nodded. "He has a debt. He's trying to pay it off. It's for gambling. It's bad. He took out a couple of loans with some bad guys back home, and now they want it back. I was worried about him, and that's why I agreed to help him. He said he thought he could win it back in the ship's casino. I was just trying to help him. But then he... started talking all this nonsense about the missing children and how we could get money from the parents and stuff, and I didn't know what to do. He wanted me to give the mom a letter, but I couldn't. He kept saying I would get rich if I helped him. I didn't know he would... that he had killed that little girl. It makes me sick to think of it."

"Why would he kill her if he wanted to ransom the children?" I asked.

She shrugged. "I don't know. Maybe it was an accident?"

I nodded. It sounded plausible.

"But you saw the older girl, you say?" I asked.

She nodded again and pointed at the bed. "She was right there in the bed, sleeping. I saw her feet sticking out from under the covers and knew it had to be her. It scared me so much because that's when I realized it, you know? That my brother, my own flesh and blood, that he had... he had hurt that little girl. I told him I would go to the police, and he tried to stop me. But then that guy... that guy came running toward me and grabbed me and you... you... I almost died. You could have missed, you know? Shot me in the face instead."

"I don't miss," I said. "Never have, never will."

She gave me a look of concern. "But still."

"Back to your brother," I said. "I need you to keep focused here. Where is he now? And more importantly, you said the girl was here, alive. Where is she now?"

Elena looked at me, then shrugged. "I don't know. After talking to you upstairs, we came back here, and she was gone."

"Had he taken her somewhere else?"

She shook her head. "I don't think so."

"Are you sure? Could he have somewhere else he would hide her? Another room onboard, maybe? Is there anyone else he knows or has gotten to know?"

She shook her head. "I don't know. But I don't think he moved her."

"And why is that?"

"Because he panicked when he found out she was gone. He said he gave her sleeping pills in her drink, but she didn't drink it. She just pretended to."

"Smart girl," I said and looked up at Dana. I rose to my feet. "She escaped."

"But that means she's out there somewhere," Dana said. "All by herself?"

I nodded. "And we need to find her before he does."

Part V

SUNDAY 6 P.M.

Chapter 58

"I'M TELLING YOU, a bunch of people are talking about doing it. They've created a Facebook group and everything."

"That doesn't mean we have to get involved, does it?"

The woman with the long blonde hair and soft curls looked up at her husband.

He nodded. "Yes, we should. The more of us who show up and stand up to these people, the better the chances of us getting somewhere. They can't keep us locked up on this ship forever. It's unconstitutional."

Becky looked at the boy sitting next to her on the pool deck. The boy couldn't be much older than her younger sister Nicky. The thought of her sister made her sad. She felt a pinch in the depth of her stomach when remembering her. She stared at the boy. He was playing with two plastic trucks that his mom had brought. Becky looked around anxiously, hoping no one would notice her. She had been playing with this boy for a long time now, hoping that her being with this family would help hide her. She was pretending like she was part of the family.

"Yeah, you're right," the boy's mother said. "We really shouldn't just sit here and take it. We paid an awful lot for these tickets, and they won't even let us go see the island. I'm sick of being on this ship. It's not like we can run away. It's an island."

"Exactly. They can't do this to us," the dad said with a snort. "I say we demonstrate our rights and just walk off the ship. What are they going to do to us? Shoot us? For leaving the ship? They can't do that."

The lady's voice on the speakers interrupted them, telling them that the trivia game was starting in the inside sports bar, and then she listed all the other activities planned for the evening.

"...and once again, we thank you all for your patience through this...."

"See?" the dad said. "They're not planning on letting us off this ship at all. They will have activities planned all night, and then tomorrow morning, we'll take off and go home. No private island, no drinks on the sandy beach, no waterpark."

"They can't do that," the mom said. "We paid a lot of money for this."

"Exactly."

Becky listened in as they spoke while biting her nails. She saw crew members walking past and hid her face behind the big father's hairy back. She had thought about approaching one of them and asking for help, but she didn't dare to. She had seen that the man who held her captive was with one of them, and she didn't trust them. What if they took her back to him?

No, she had to keep hiding.

"Where's your mom and dad, sweetie?"

It took a few seconds before Becky realized the mom was talking to her. "Eh, they're right over there," Becky said and pointed at a random couple. "In the lounge chairs on the other side."

The mom stared at her. "Why are you in your PJs and not your swimsuit, little girl?"

Becky looked down at herself, then laughed. "I didn't want to change. My mom got really mad."

That made the mom laugh. "Oh, we know how that goes."

"Yeah," Becky said, not quite understanding what she meant.

"But you should probably head on back to your parents now," the mom said and folded a shirt before she put it back in her bag. "We're about to take off now. But thanks for playing with Tommy. It was very nice of you."

The mom rose to her feet and reached out her hand. "Come on, Tommy-boy. Say goodbye to the nice girl."

Tommy waved, and Becky waved back anxiously. As the parents disappeared, so did her cover.

Chapter 59

THEN:

"Sweetie, please sit down. We need to talk."

Bryan looked at Tina. She was standing in the doorway to the kitchen. Her eyes grew wide.

"What is this?"

"Just, please come in and sit down," he said.

"Darryl and Bette? What are you two doing here?" she asked, her voice trembling slightly.

"We're worried about you," Bette said. She looked briefly at Bryan, and their eyes met before she turned to look at Tina again. "We're very concerned and wanted to support Bryan when he confronted you."

"What is this... some sort of intervention?" Tina almost hissed.

Darryl nodded. "Yeah, you could call it that."

"So, now you're all... what? Plotting against me?"

"See, that's exactly the kind of stuff we're worried about," Bryan said. "You're acting very paranoid, and it's destroying our family."

Tina stared at him, then shook her head. "I don't believe you. Why would you humiliate me like this?"

"Tina, you need help," Bette said.

"Professional help," Bryan added.

Tina scoffed. "You're all crazy."

"We think you might be losing it, Tina," Bette said.

"You used to be my friend," Tina said and pointed at her.

"I still am."

Tina narrowed her eyes. "You're all brainwashed, don't you see? If you can't see the dangers we're facing right now, then I can't help you."

"What dangers are they exactly?"

A woman stepped out into the kitchen.

"Who's she?" Tina asked.

"This is Dr. Lawson. She is an expert in treating people with paranoia due to conspiracy theories," Bryan said.

Tina stepped back and stretched out her hands. "You've got to be kidding me. You brought in some shrink? And you're all in this together? Against me? Plotting this against me? How long have you been planning this, Bryan? How long?"

"That is not the topic we're discussing here," the doctor said.

Tina pointed at her. "You don't get to talk like that to me here in my house. I haven't invited you here, so would you please leave?"

"She can help you," Bryan said.

Tina touched her head with both hands. "Can't you all hear how crazy that sounds? Help me? Help me with what?"

"Get better," Bette said. "Dr. Lawson runs this facility that…."

"You're trying to put me away?" Tina shrieked. "Have you all lost your minds? You want to get rid of me?"

"No one is trying to…." Bryan walked toward her, but Tina moved back. "Don't you touch me. I can't even look at you right now. Then she turned around and stormed out. She rushed up the stairs, ran into the children's bedroom, and locked the door.

Chapter 60

"HAVE YOU SEEN THIS GIRL?"

I showed a woman my phone with the recent picture of Becky that her dad had given to me. Dana was with me, doing the same. I had told the captain to have all his crew members look for the girl. It was obvious that he was getting tired of it all, and he sighed, annoyed when I asked him to start another search.

"My superiors are on my back because of this," he said. "Passengers are calling in and complaining. We tried to search the ship. It's no use. There are just too many places to hide. I need to let people off the ship soon if I am to keep my job."

"Just give me a little more time," I said. "The girl is alive and somewhere on this ship. If we start to let people leave, she might get lost with them, and we will never find her. Also, the killer is on the ship, too, trying to find her. I need your crew members to keep an eye out for him as well."

I showed him the picture of Travis, and he agreed—even though it was reluctantly—to conduct another search.

"But you can't bother the passengers," he said. "We're trying to keep a good atmosphere here and pretend everything is okay.

It's what we do. We keep up the good atmosphere and make people feel like everything is just fine even if the darn boat is sinking."

Captain Larsen had raised his voice at that last bit, and I knew he was about to lose it. He was a very calm man with a calm demeanor through most situations, as he had shown me up until now. But it was clear that now he was about to lose it.

I couldn't blame him. The pressure was on.

The woman I showed the picture to shook her head, then walked on. Dana talked to a young couple with a stroller. They, too, shook their heads. I exchanged a look with Dana and noticed she was sweating heavily. Her short curly hair had gotten tousled, and the look in her eyes was exhaustion. I couldn't blame her. I felt the same way. But I couldn't give up now—not when we were this close. I knew Becky was here somewhere. And I knew she had to be close. I felt it.

I just didn't understand why she didn't walk up to a crew member and tell them who she was. It could be anyone—a waitress at one of the restaurants, a cleaning lady, or maybe even a....

But she won't because she knows that the people who kept her locked up were members of the crew. She saw Elena and knew. This girl is too smart to make that mistake. Of course, she is.

"This guy says he saw a young girl on the top deck," Dana said, coming up to me.

"He couldn't say it was the exact same girl, but...."

Dana paused as a tall guy came toward us, raising his arm. "Hey, you. Yes, you two."

"Excuse me?" I asked and turned around to face him. He walked closer to Dana and got in her face.

"I want to know how long you're gonna keep us locked up," he said. "We're all getting a little tired of this."

"I understand, sir, but...," Dana started, but he interrupted her. He was a big guy and becoming threatening in his attitude.

"We are all here getting our vacation ruined; do you realize that?" he continued. "We didn't do anything wrong. It's not our fault."

"Sir, I'm gonna need you to take a step back…."

He didn't react but continued unabated.

"You can't keep us here against our will. It's not right."

A crowd had started to gather behind him, mostly other big guys just like him, and I didn't like the situation. Dana was holding up a hand to stop him from getting closer.

"Sir, we're working on solving this matter as soon as possible. I'm just asking for your patience."

He threw out his arms. He was wearing a blue tank top that said, *SURELY NOT EVERYONE WAS KUNG FU FIGHTING?*

"Patience? Patience?" he said, raising his voice. "We've been here for hours now. We can't even leave the ship. It's driving us nuts. We paid a lot of money for this; I sure hope the cruise line is planning on reimbursing us. You see to it that they do."

"Not quite my department, but I'm sure they will…."

He pointed his finger at her, placing it very close to her face. "You better. People are about to revolt here."

"Again, we're just asking for your patience…."

"We've been patient enough, am I right?"

The crowd behind him agreed. I placed a hand on my weapon. More people were approaching and started to yell at us.

"This is a free country. We're Americans. You can't just keep us locked up like this. We're not the criminals here."

Again, the crowd agreed.

"Sir, you need to step back," Dana said, her voice growing stern.

"Or what? You'll arrest me?"

"Yes, that is exactly what I will do."

"For what? Executing my rights? You'll have to arrest all of us, then."

He pointed at the crowd behind him, who again agreed in unison.

I stepped closer to Dana so she knew I was with her. "Sir," I said. "You were asked kindly to take a step back."

"And what if I don't want to? I'm sick of being told what to do. I didn't do anything wrong."

The crowd moved closer, and I was beginning to feel claustrophobic. I looked away for a second because I spotted movement behind the crowd, and suddenly I saw a little girl as she ran into the elevator. The big guy from earlier pushed Dana, and she stumbled back.

I pulled my gun.

"Enough of this!"

That was a language they understood. They paused when seeing the gun. I gave them the look my teenagers usually got when I was done with all their nonsense. It worked. They backed off.

"Everyone, go to your rooms."

"Excuse me?" someone said.

I lost it. I admit I did. I'm not proud of it, but it happened. I yelled at them, "You heard me. You're interrupting police business. I want everyone in their rooms now! GO!"

Chapter 61

"YOU'RE TELLING me you know where my daughter is?"

Travis looked up at Bryan McCarthy. He was such a big guy; it was frightening. He would much rather have dealt with the mom than the dad. But since she didn't believe him, it left him only one option.

"Y-yes."

Bryan narrowed his eyes. They had met in the bathroom by the elevators. Travis had paid a waitress who was taking Bryan food to sneak in the letter with the sandwich, telling him to meet him there.

"And you have the nerve to come and tell me?" he asked.

"What do you mean?"

He leaned forward. "Why didn't you tell the police?"

"Because I want money. And you're loaded. Everyone knows that."

Bryan stared down at him, then moved a step closer. Travis was sweating heavily, and his heart rate was going up. This guy could beat him up right now, and no one would know. It was risky.

"You're saying that you want money to give me back my daughter."

He nodded. "Yes. Three million… no, make that four."

Bryan scoffed. "And she's alive?"

"Yes. Very much alive."

"So, how do I know you're telling the truth? You could be some random guy just trying to get money out of us."

"You'll just have to trust me." He pulled out the hair tie and showed it to him. Bryan looked at it, then nodded.

"I'm gonna need more than that."

Travis closed his eyes briefly. Why wouldn't they just believe him when he told them?

"Okay, so what do you need? Pictures?" he asked.

Bryan bit the side of his cheek, then crossed his arms in front of his chest. "You bring me my girl, and I will pay you. But I need to see the girl."

Travis looked at him and smiled. Then, he nodded.

"Okay, meet me here in an hour."

"Thirty minutes," Bryan said. "If you really do have her, it shouldn't take more than that."

Travis swallowed hard. He couldn't really tell him that he had lost her. He would have to find her.

Bryan leaned close to his face. "Be back here in half an hour with the girl, and I will transfer the money to your bank account, and no one will know. If not, the police will get involved, and you're a dead man."

Travis nodded. He reached out his hand.

"Deal."

Bryan McCarthy didn't shake it. He just glared down at it, then shook his head and walked past him.

"You better have her and bring her."

"Of course," Travis said as he watched Bryan McCarthy disappear through the door. Then he leaned against the sink and looked at his reflection and the sweat running down his temples while whispering under his breath, "It's just one little girl. How hard can it be to find her?"

Chapter 62

THEN:

Bryan hammered on the door. He felt so helpless because the kids were in there with her. Were they okay?

"Tina? It's me. Please, open the door."

"No," she said. "I don't want to talk to any of you. You ambushed me."

Bryan sighed. "Please, Tina. Don't do this. We didn't mean to scare you. We were only trying to help."

"No, you're trying to get rid of me," Tina said. "You want me put away. I won't let you."

"You're being paranoid again. No one wants to harm you in any way. Just open the door, and we can talk about this."

"So you can have them take me away?" Tina said. "I'm not that stupid."

Bryan rubbed his temples. "Who are *they* and *them* you are talking about? It's just you and me and the kids here now. Everyone else left."

She went quiet. "I don't believe you."

"Of course, you don't. Why would you?" he said with a deep

exhale. "You never believe anything I say. Only those stupid web pages and the YouTube videos that you keep watching. Am I not more important than them?"

"You tricked me. You brought in a doctor. You want me diagnosed and put away," she said. "Don't think I don't see what you're doing here."

"But…," he paused, tired. They went silent for a few minutes. Bryan could hear their youngest, Nicky, crying on the other side of the door.

"Are the children okay?"

"Yes, they're fine," Tina said. "They're with their mom as they should be. If you send me away, who will take care of them?"

"Daddy? Daddy?" Becky said, her voice trembling. "Why won't Mommy let you in? I'm scared."

"It's okay, sweetie. Mom and Dad are just talking," he said. He closed his eyes briefly, trying to figure out what to do next—how to handle this situation. He had to get Tina out of that room before she did something irrational.

"Okay, okay," he said. "I'll admit that it was a little too much having all those people here, the whole intervention thing. It was excessive. And I'm sorry if that scared you."

She didn't say anything, so he continued.

"But I didn't know what else to do. I'm at the end of my rope here, Tina. I don't know how to help you."

"I don't need your help. You're the one who needs help."

He sighed again. "I don't need help. I'm not the one who thinks the entire world is plotting against me."

She went quiet for a few minutes before she said.

"You're one of them, aren't you?"

"What do you mean?"

"The reptiles. You're one of them. You have been all along."

"Excuse me?"

"It all makes sense now. You're one of them, and that means so are our children."

213

Chapter 63

I WATCHED the girl through the glass in the elevator as she soared upward inside the ship toward the top floor. My eyes locked with hers as she stared down at us, hands leaning on the glass.

"It's her."

"What's that?" Dana asked.

The crowd had finally broken up, and people were walking away. Some of them were still mumbling angry slurs at us while shaking their heads. I paid no attention to them as I was occupied with watching the girl.

Becky.

I pointed at the elevator, my heart rate going up. "It's her. It's Becky."

"What?" Dana looked in the direction I was pointing. She shook her head. "I don't see her."

"In the elevator. The one to the left."

I didn't have time to wait for her to see what I was seeing. I needed to get into another elevator and get up there before she disappeared again.

"Trust me; it's definitely her. Get help," I said and took off running. I reached the elevators and must have pressed the button a hundred times.

"Come on; come on."

The elevator dinged, and one opened up behind me. I turned to walk toward it when someone beat me to it. He came from out of nowhere, stormed inside, and pressed the button.

"Hey!"

I reached out my hand to stop it, but the doors closed fast, and just as they did, I recognized him.

Travis Gasgarth.

"No!"

I pressed the button again and again, then realized it was taking too long. Travis was going for the girl, and he was ahead of me. I needed to get to the top floor fast. I looked around and spotted the stairs.

I took two steps at a time, then cursed myself for eating all that junk food I had been munching on, especially the Reese's Peanut Butter Cups I couldn't stay away from these days.

You can do this, Eva Rae. You can make it.

It was eight floors up to the top, and by the time I finally made it up there, Travis was nowhere to be seen. Neither was Becky.

On the other hand, I was panting, agitated, and wheezing like that penguin toy in the second *Toy Story* movie.

It was bad.

I went out on the sundeck and scanned the area, then spotted the girl as she was walking around the corner toward the pool. I followed her, running again.

"Hey, Becky. Stop."

I rounded the corner and arrived at the pool deck, where I was greeted by hundreds of passengers that had gathered there. They were all yelling and screaming angry words while someone was riling them up by yelling on a megaphone.

"We want to get off the ship! You can't keep us here! We are not criminals!"

I kept my eyes on the girl as I spotted her zigzagging through the crowd between people's legs. I went after her, trying to yell her name, but was drowned out by the crowd's yelling.

I spotted her between some legs as she reached the bar area. I elbowed my way through the mob while people scolded me loudly. I made it to the bar area but couldn't see her anymore.

"Where did she go?" I mumbled, looking all around me.

That's when I saw her standing by the clean towels.

"Becky!"

Our eyes locked again as I leaped toward her, but some big woman stepped out in front of me and got in my way. Once I managed to get around her, Becky was gone.

Where did she go?

I looked around me again just in time to see her. She was being dragged across the deck, a hand covering her mouth.

Travis's hand.

Chapter 64

TRAVIS PULLED the girl toward the elevators. He couldn't believe his luck. He had walked right out of that bathroom, thinking there was no way he could find the girl in just half an hour, and then he saw her get into that elevator.

That kind of stuff just didn't happen.

At least not to Travis.

"Shh," he whispered. "I'm getting you back to your parents. I'm trying to do what is right."

The girl was fighting his grip, trying to scream behind his hand and hitting him with her elbows.

"I spoke to them, and I'm taking you back to them now."

But the girl didn't seem to believe him. The more he spoke, the more aggressively she tried to fight him. So instead, he grabbed her by the waist, put her on his shoulder, and then ran toward the elevators, praying no one would take notice. The girl was screaming and yelling, but luckily, the rally that had been arranged on the top deck was way louder, and no one could hear her, nor did they take any notice.

They were way too busy getting riled up and angry at the cruise line for keeping them hostage.

Again, luck was in Travis's favor as he ran to the elevators, and one was left open. He stormed inside and pressed the button.

"Put me down, you creep," the girl yelled while kicking and hitting him.

"Just a few more floors," he said as the elevator darted downward. He was breaking into a sweat from carrying the girl and probably from all the anxiety he was feeling.

But soon, it would be all over.

And he would be a rich man.

The bell rang, and the doors opened to the floor where he would meet the man with all the money. Travis could barely contain his joy. After all this work, he deserved to have a win. He deserved to get a massive load of money. No one could say he had come to it easily.

But the rest of his life was going to be easy.

As soon as he paid off all his debt, he would still have enough money to live the rest of his life.

Of course, he was going to gamble a little here and there. But just for the fun of it, not because he needed the money anymore. Nope. Those days were over.

Travis carried the girl out on the first floor and spotted the bathroom by the exits to the gangways. FBI agents guarded all entrances and exits, so no one would leave the ship, and he had to be careful that none of them saw him with the girl. This was going to be tricky. He had to get to the bathroom door and inside where the dad would meet him soon. But carrying a screaming girl on his shoulder would look suspicious.

He put her down, then placed a hand over her mouth. He looked into her eyes sternly.

"Listen to me, little girl. Your dad is waiting inside that bathroom over there. I will take you to him, but you must remain calm. No yelling."

Her eyes grew wide, and she was panting loudly behind the hand, almost hyperventilating.

"Can you do that? I don't want to have to hurt you."

She stared at him, and he took that as a yes. Carefully, he let go of her mouth and waited to see her reaction.

She didn't scream.

"Okay, let's go."

He turned the corner, holding a hand on the girl's neck, pressing down so she would remember that he was right there and could hurt her if he wanted to. Not that he would ever hurt her; he was way too soft for that, but she didn't know that.

"Right in here," he said with a smile directed at the agents who were standing not far away. He led the girl through the door, then closed it behind him.

The bathroom was empty.

The dad wasn't there. At least not yet.

Travis looked at his watch. There were still a few minutes left, so it was all good.

He splashed some water on his face, then looked at his reflection when he heard the door open and footsteps approach.

Travis didn't turn to look yet, but said, "You're right on time."

He was about to turn his head and look at the person who had entered when something hard hit him on the back of the neck, and all he saw were stars.

Chapter 65

I RAN to the elevators and saw that Travis had stopped on the first floor. I made it down the stairs again, thinking it would be faster than the elevator, but the crowds had begun to move from the top deck and were blocking not only the elevators but also the stairs, so it took longer than I thought it would. I pushed people aside, telling them I was with the FBI, holding up my badge, but they didn't move.

It was beyond frustrating.

I couldn't see Travis or Becky anywhere when I reached the first floor. I stopped and scanned the area just as the men's bathroom door opened, and someone came running out.

Becky!

"What the…?"

She stopped right when she stepped outside, and our eyes locked again for just a brief second.

Then the deck surrounding us started to shake.

"What is going on?"

We both stood like we were frozen as the trembling continued, and I realized too late what was about to happen. I turned to look behind me, and that's when I knew.

A stampede!

That's exactly what it sounded like, at least—like horses or cows stampeding. Except it wasn't animals. It was humans. I couldn't believe my eyes as I watched what was probably around a thousand passengers head for the exit, storming it. They were trampling and pushing any obstacle in their way, whether it was a decorative flower arrangement, a glass table, or a crew member trying to stop them. Even the FBI agents guarding the exits jumped to the side to get out of their way. I was pushed down by a flock of women in their swimsuits and landed on the floor, hitting my head on the marble tiles. I gasped for air, slightly panicking while trying to get up, but I kept getting pushed back down. I managed to lift my head just enough to be able to look between the many legs.

Somewhere in there, I spotted Becky as she was flooded by the crowd and soon lifted by the pressure and pushed in the direction they were going. The stampede went through the fence blocking the exit with a loud crash and many cheering voices. They pushed their way down the ramp. With them, they took Becky, and the last I saw of her, she was getting an elbow in her face, and seconds later, she was pushed over the railing and fell off the edge of the gangway.

Chapter 66

"NO-NO-NO-NO!"

Everything stopped as the girl fell over the railing. Each and every crazy stampeding and running passenger instantly stopped what they were doing and froze in place.

It was surreal to watch.

As fast as possible, I got up. I made my way through the crowd toward the ramp and looked down. There she was, in the water, her back turned to us, bobbing up and down.

Please, don't be dead, please!

Two men that had seen it happen were already at the dock. One jumped in the water. He pulled Becky toward the seawall, and the other guy helped him pull her out. More came to help, and soon they had Becky completely out of the water. I elbowed my way down the gangway.

"Coming through. Coming through."

I watched as one man began performing CPR on the girl, and my heart started to drum inside my chest. I approached them and knelt next to her.

"She just… she just… fell," one of the men said. He was tearing up as he realized what he had been a part of. "We just… we just wanted to get to the island and…."

I pushed away the man doing CPR and continued where he left off. People behind me were crying and staring helplessly into the air.

"Get the medical officers from the infirmary," I said. "Quick."

Someone took off running.

"Is she breathing?" the first man asked while I compressed her chest. There was still no pulse. I tried again.

"Is she… alive?" he asked.

I felt for a pulse once more. Then, I nodded, relief rushing over me.

"I got a pulse."

"Oh, thank God," he answered.

The medical officers came fast, put her on a stretcher, and then took her back into the infirmary at the ship. I wasn't happy to leave her again, but I knew she would be in good hands.

I called Dana and asked her to get the girl's parents to come down and be with her. Meanwhile, I rushed into the men's bathroom to see what—or rather who—the girl was running from. In there, I saw Travis Gasgarth. He was on the floor, blood seeping from the back of his head and onto the floor. I called for help, and soon, two FBI agents came to help me get him to his feet. He moaned something, then touched the back of his head.

"What happened?"

"You're under arrest for the murder of Nicky McCarthy and the kidnapping of Becky McCarthy," I said. "That's what happening. You have the right to remain sil…."

He looked up at me. "Wait, what?"

"You heard me."

"But wait a minute," he said and shook his head. "I didn't kill anyone."

"They all say that," one of the FBI agents said with a smirk.

"But it's true," he said.

"They all say that too."

"No, no, you're not listening to me," he said. "The young girl was already dead."

The two agents laughed, but I was suddenly listening.

"What do you mean?"

"I went into their room to… well, steal some cash, and that's when I saw them in the bathroom—the two little girls. The youngest was dead—I checked her for a pulse and everything. The oldest was looking at me with those big eyes of hers. I took her because I wanted to help her—to save her from whoever had hurt her sister and was obviously going to do the same to her. She was crying and scared."

"But wait, that makes no sense," I said. "Your sister said you took them to blackmail for money."

"That was later," he said. "I mean, I came up with that idea later. Okay, so, to be perfectly honest, maybe I didn't take her to save her. I figured that if I took her with me, whoever had hurt her sister would know I knew what they had done and would pay me. There. I thought I could make some money. Pay off my debt. Move on with my life."

"Nice try. I'm still booking you," I said and nodded at the agents to take him to the detention area below deck. I sensed he was telling the truth, and it bugged me. I would need to get all this figured out, but how?

My head was spinning. I couldn't get the pieces to fall into place. Did this mean that it was, after all, Gerard Hutcheon who had murdered the girl?

What was I missing?

That's when Dana called for me over the radio. "FBI Agent Thomas. I need to talk to you."

Chapter 67

THEN:

Bryan ran to the kitchen and grabbed his phone. He dialed nine-one-one.

"Hello? I need someone to come to my house. I think my wife is about to hurt our children."

It didn't take long before two police cars raced up into their driveway. Bryan opened the gate for them and let them into the house.

"She's barricaded herself upstairs in the children's bedroom."

"And the children, sir?"

"She's got them with her."

"Show me the way, please."

Bryan hurried up the stairs, the two officers right behind him. He walked to the door and placed a hand on it.

"They're in here. I'm scared of what she might do to them."

"And why is that, sir?"

Bryan stared at the officer. He hesitated to answer. Would it sound too crazy if he told them the truth? That his wife thought her husband and children were reptiles? Would anyone believe that?

"Because she is not well," he said, trying to avoid it. "She thinks everyone is out to hurt her."

The officer looked at him. "Are they?"

Suddenly, Bryan could see how this looked. "Listen, Officer; I'm not... I haven't tried to... she's the one who is threatening to harm the children."

"Did she threaten to do that? Did you hear her say she would harm the children?" he asked.

"Not in those words, but she said that...."

"That what?"

He swallowed. He could tell the officer didn't believe him. "I know what this looks like. But that's not what it is."

"And what is that exactly, sir?"

He felt trapped. How could he explain it so this man would believe him?

"It looks like I... like I was after her, and she barricaded herself in the room with the children to protect them and won't come out. But I am telling you, that's not what happened. I have not hurt her nor had any intention to do so."

"Okay, then you won't mind if we ask her ourselves?"

"No, of course not. Go ahead."

The officer knocked on the door. "Ma'am? This is Officer Burns with GBPD. Are you okay in there?"

She didn't answer. The silence made Bryan nervous. "I'm telling you, there is something wrong."

The two officers looked at one another. The first one knocked again, this time even harder.

"Ma'am, please open the door."

Still nothing. The officer shook his head.

"This isn't right."

He looked at his colleague, then used his shoulder to break down the door. It swung open and slammed against the wall behind it.

Bryan went in first, even though the officers told him to wait.

As soon as he stepped inside, he spotted Tina. She was bent over their youngest in the bed, her hands wrapped around the little girl's throat.

Chapter 68

I TOOK the stairs to the bridge, where Dana was waiting for me. Kent Black, the medical examiner, was with her. They both turned to face me when I entered.

"Agent Thomas," Dana said and approached. "Kent has something he needs to tell you."

She nodded at the small man standing next to her. "Go ahead. Tell her what you told me."

He cleared his throat and looked at the file he was holding between his hands. "Yes, remember how you asked me to take a look at Tina McCarthy's bruises to determine whether or not they could be self-inflicted?"

I nodded. "Yes?"

"Well, I had to analyze the findings for quite some time to be certain, at least enough to give you my expert opinion, but…."

He cleared his throat again.

"Yes?" I said, trying to get him to get to the point. Patience wasn't one of my strong suits. "And were they?"

He exhaled. "It's a gray area we're approaching here since it's hard to say exactly in these matters."

"But what is your conclusion?"

He nodded and pushed his glasses back up on his nose. "Yes, they could possibly be self-inflicted. I'm not saying that they are, but it is possible, yes."

"How?" I asked.

"Well, I believe the bruises on her neck stem from what I believe is a belt. They're not made by fingers, and they're not deep enough nor severe enough to actually kill anyone. They're very superficial."

"Let me get this straight. You're saying she tried to hang herself, but chickened out, then decided to jump instead?" I asked, looking briefly at Dana. "Is that what you're saying? That she tried to kill herself?"

He tilted his head. "That is one possibility, yes. With the way the pressure points are located…."

I placed a hand on his arm. "She did a terrible job of it. Thank you very much."

He smiled, slightly dissatisfied. It was obvious he wanted to explain it to me in more detail, but I was running out of time. He nodded, then left.

"There's more," Dana said and handed me her phone. "This just came to our attention."

I scrolled through the email. "What's this?"

"A police report. Filed a little over a year ago."

I looked up at her. "Tina was arrested? Why have I not heard of this before?"

"It didn't come up at first because they didn't press charges since they couldn't prove anything."

"But a domestic disturbance? And she threatened to kill her children because she believed they were… reptiles?"

Dana exhaled. "It's a thing, a conspiracy theory that is pretty well out there. It's the idea that this world is controlled by aliens who came here many years ago—that they live among us. Supposedly, they are these blood-drinking, flesh-eating, shape-shifting extraterrestrial reptilian humanoids who just want to enslave the human race. According to the people who believe in this stuff, these reptiles are everywhere, especially among our political leaders and Hollywood superstars."

"I have heard about that, but your own children? It says here she had her hands around the youngest's throat?"

"Yes, that is in the husband's statement. But she told the officers that she was just caressing the child. The officers on the scene didn't see her do it because when they came into the room after the husband, her hands weren't touching the child anymore. There were no bruises on the child's neck. That's why the charges were dropped."

"We need to talk to her. Where is she now?"

Dana looked at me nervously. "Well, you told me to take her to see Becky in the infirmary below deck, so I did. Becky is still unconscious, and she needs her mother. She's in there with her now."

Chapter 69

THE DOOR to the infirmary was closed when we got there, and the nurses and doctor were waiting outside. They were talking to Bryan McCarthy, but the talking stopped as we approached them.

"Is she in there?" I asked and pointed at the door.

The doctor nodded. "We thought we would give them some privacy. The child is still unconscious."

"And she's alone with her mother?" I asked.

He nodded. I stormed past him and grabbed the door handle. He yelled after me, "We called the hospital in Nassau, and they're sending a coast guard chopper."

"By then, it might be too late," I said and opened the door, one hand resting on the grip of my gun as I entered.

Inside, I spotted Tina. She was sitting by the child's bedside, her head on her chest, crying. Becky had gotten an IV drip in her hand but had still not opened her eyes. I felt relieved when seeing that I wasn't too late.

"My baby, my poor baby," Tina said, sobbing.

I approached her and placed a hand on her shoulder. "Tina?"

She looked up, her eyes bloodshot. "Y-yes?"

"We need to talk."

"O-of course," she said. She looked briefly at her daughter. "Can we do it here? I don't want to leave my daughter."

"I would rather do it someplace else," I said.

Her eyes begged me. "I'm not leaving her."

She sniffled and wiped her nose with a tissue.

"What's going on?"

It was Bryan who had come in. He stood in the doorway, looking at us.

"I just need to talk to your wife," I said.

"What's it about?" Tina asked. "You can say anything to me here. I don't care."

I swallowed. I was hoping to get her on my own. But Bryan was going to find out sooner or later anyway, so I guessed now was as good a time as ever.

"You failed to tell us that you were recently arrested for threatening to hurt your children," I said. "We just got the police report."

She nodded and sniffled again. "Yeah, I thought that might come up. But I wasn't sure since they never charged me with anything."

"Just because they couldn't prove it," Bryan said and came closer. "What are you saying, Agent Thomas? You think my wife hurt Nicky and Becky?"

His eyes grew wild, and I knew I had to tread carefully.

"We don't know," I said. "But I would like to know about your suicide attempt when you jumped in the ocean."

Her eyes grew wide. "No. It wasn't a suicide attempt. Someone pushed me into the water."

"She's lying, isn't she?" Bryan said, his tone growing increasingly angry. "I knew I saw her try to strangle Nicky that day. That's what I told the police. And they believed me. You yelled at them, remember? You called them all reptiles. They believed *me*. But they couldn't prove anything, and since Nicky wasn't harmed, there wasn't anything to press charges about."

"Tina," I said. "I need you to be honest with us now for your own good. We understand that accidents happen and that people snap from time to time. Fear, paranoia, call it what you want, but it can make people do crazy things, devastating things. Did you kill Nicky?"

She shook her head again. "No. No. No."

"She's lying," Bryan said. "Finally, someone is listening to me. I told you this all along. I've been trying to say this for years. She's crazy. I told the police a year ago that it was on them if she ended up killing our children. Still, they couldn't do anything, they said. I was told to give her another chance and look where that got us. My daughter is dead. Murdered. Strangled in her sleep." He pointed at Tina. "She did that with her bare hands. She killed them, or at least thought she had, because Becky somehow survived, and then… then… Tina tried to kill herself, making it look like I murdered all of them. That way, she would get me out of the way, too, and save the world from more reptiles. She was devoted to that cause. She wanted to rid the world of the monsters, beginning with our children by making sure they would never grow up to become like them. Our children, for crying out loud. My daughter, who didn't have a mean bone in her small body. I'm telling you. That's how crazy this woman is. And dangerous."

"It's not true," Tina yelled. She stood to her feet. I could tell she was confused and defeated. "It's not true. It… can't be."

I looked at her. "I'm gonna have to ask you to come with me."

She pulled away, shaking her head. "No. I can't… I can't leave her…."

I glared at Dana, who nodded. She left, then returned with two of her men. They grabbed Tina and read her rights to her, then dragged her out of the room while she screamed her daughter's name.

It was heartbreaking but necessary.

Bryan exhaled deeply when she was gone, then looked at me, tears in his eyes. "I'm just happy that someone is finally listening to me. I can't say it feels good, but at least now it's over."

Chapter 70

I HAD Tina McCarthy put in one of the detention cells below deck. I wanted to interview her as soon as possible but had to wait until she had calmed down. She was in no condition to speak to me right now. I badly needed that confession from her. The sooner, the better because then I could finally let the passengers get off the ship. They could still get a few hours on the island before the ship had to leave at ten o'clock. But most importantly, the case would be closed, and I could finish up. We could all get closure, including the father and sister.

I braced myself for more patience while I listened to Tina screaming behind the door of the detention cell. She was kicking the door now, yelling for us to open it and get her back to her daughter, who needed her.

I stepped away from the door and called Isabella. I told her everything.

"I'll be…," she said. "That's one for the books, huh?"

I exhaled heavily and grabbed a bag of chips from a cart full of snacks that someone had parked by the stairs. I was still below deck and just now walking up to the first floor to get better reception.

"You can say that again," I said as the scorching sun hit my eyes. "This is a first for me."

"I mean, I have heard about conspiracy theories destroying families and splitting marriages, but committing murder, killing your own child?" Isabella said. "That's definitely new to me. So, how far are we on the confession?"

I looked out over the endless ocean. It was breathtaking. I opened the bag of chips and started to eat.

"Working on it. But she needs to cool down first."

"Get me that confession, Eva Rae," she said. "And this will all be over."

"You know it's not that simple."

"Oh, boy, do I know," she said, laughing. "Listen, I gotta go, but keep me posted, okay? As soon as you have her on tape, you let me know."

I hung up and ate the remains of the bag of chips while thinking about this story that had been unraveled. It was a strange one, for sure. Almost too much so. There was something about it that rubbed me the wrong way, though. I couldn't figure out what it was. Yet, for some reason, I opened my phone and went through my emails, then found the phone records for Gerard Hutcheon and opened them. I knew they had come in earlier, but I hadn't had time to look through them. Something drew me to it just now, and a second later, it hit me. I stared at the last number that he had called several times.

It was a Wisconsin number.

The man was from California, as far as I knew.

Did it mean anything?

I bit the side of my cheek, wondering if it did.

Then it struck me, and I almost choked on my chips. I dropped the bag on the deck, then ran for the stairs, gun pulled.

I screwed up. Oh, my God, I screwed up!

Chapter 71

BECKY DIDN'T KNOW where she was at first. She felt dizzy—like she was half asleep, half awake, then blinked her eyes to figure out which one it was.

Then, she remembered.

She gasped for air and opened her eyes widely. A face appeared in front of her, and she couldn't breathe as she looked into his eyes.

"There you are, sweetie," he said.

"D-Dad?"

"You were in an accident," he said.

She shook her head desperately as he came closer.

"N-no. Please, Dad. No."

He smiled. "It's gonna be just fine, honey. Just lay back down now."

"Please, Daddy, please."

He tilted his head. "It will only take a second. Then, it's all over. Just remain calm, okay?"

"Where is Mom? D-Daddy? Where is Mommy?" Becky said, feeling panic as it rushed through her small body. She tried to sit up, but he pushed her back down. Then, she cried.

"Shh. There's no reason to cry," he said. "It will be all over soon."

He lifted the pillow he was holding between his hands and placed it on top of her, then put all his weight on it. Everything went dark for Becky, and the more she tried to scream and move around, the harder it became for her to breathe. Soon, she was gasping for air, and her body was jolting in spasms.

Chapter 72

I ALMOST FELL down the stairs; that's how fast I was going. I stormed to the infirmary, where the doctor and nurses all looked up from their computers and phones as I screamed at them.

"Is he in there? Is he in there?"

"Is who in where?" the doctor said.

"Bryan McCarthy, is he in there... alone with Becky?" I panted.

The doctor nodded, and I didn't wait for him to say anything before I ran for the door and pulled it open. I held the gun between my hands and stepped inside.

"Stop it right there, Bryan. It's over."

He was bent over Becky's small body, crying.

"I think she... I think she died," he said. "The... fall... the water... it was too much. She didn't make it."

I stared at the little girl in the bed. I was barely able to breathe.

Had I come too late?

I saw the pillow on the chair next to the bed.

"Get down," I said. "Get down on your knees with your arms above your head."

"Agent Thomas?" he said, surprised. "But... why? Don't you see my daughter... she's... dead."

"Arms above your head," I said. "I need you flat on the floor."

He did as I told him and laid down. I hurried to Becky's body, my heart racing in my chest.

Oh, dear God, no. Please, don't let her be dead!

I placed two fingers on her throat and felt a pulse. I breathed, relieved, when she opened her eyes.

"Oh, dear God, Becky. Are you okay?"

She nodded. "I did the same as I did when he tried to kill me in our room. I just pretended. Then, he stopped."

I clasped my chest. "You pretended to be dead? Oh, you clever, clever girl. That's how you survived. When he dragged you and your sister into the bathroom and left you there, he thought you were both dead. He went out to find the perfect spot to get rid of your bodies. Your mom was already in the water, but it had to look like she killed the children and then herself, so he needed somewhere else for the children."

She nodded cautiously. "Is he gone?"

I looked at the floor, then saw him just as he wormed his way toward the door, probably hoping I wouldn't see him. I walked up to him and placed my sneaker on his back.

"You're not going anywhere, mister. I'm taking you in."

I grabbed him by the hair and pulled his head up.

"Do you know where you messed up? When you said your daughter was strangled in her sleep, using bare hands. We haven't told anyone about that yet, and only someone who was there could know. That was the one mistake you made, and you can think about that for the rest of your life as you spend it behind bars for killing your own daughter. I can't help wondering how deep a panic you must have felt when coming back and realizing that Becky was gone. You thought you killed them both and your wife too. But they outsmarted you. You must have been so scared of getting caught; I can't even imagine. And all this was for what purpose? Because you had a stupid affair? You wanted to start over. Create a new family? Am I right?"

I didn't wait for an answer. I knew I was right. I could see it in his eyes.

Then, I cuffed him.

Epilogue
TWO DAYS LATER

"IT WAS his brother's wife he was having an affair with. Can you believe it?"

"Dear God," Dana said and looked at me.

I was holding balloons and flowers in my hands as we walked up the hallway of Princess Margaret's Hospital in Nassau.

It was two days later, and I had been working on finishing my report while living in a hotel on solid ground in the Bahamian capital. I was almost ready to go back home, but I wanted to check on Becky first.

"I know it's crazy, right? He was seeing her on the side, and the two of them planned the whole thing. They decided to use the fact that Tina was into conspiracy theories to make her seem crazy enough to harm the children, but she never was. She never said she would hurt them. They made that part up."

"But she did believe that Bryan was a reptile, right?"

I tilted my head. "He sure was a monster, all right. She wasn't completely off."

That made Dana laugh.

"But it didn't work the first time they tried," I said. "At the house, when they called the police on her after their so-called intervention freaked her out. That's when they decided to do the cruise plan. In a place with many people and many cameras that could show how much she was drinking. They needed to make sure they had enough evidence of her erratic behavior. That's also why Bryan made her believe beforehand that he had an affair—to make sure she freaked out. And if that wasn't enough, they hired a photographer to document the entire thing—to make sure there were pictures taken of Tina drinking and acting irrationally."

"Gerard Hutcheon?" Dana asked.

"Exactly. A well-known paparazzi who will do anything for money. But he made the mistake of calling Bryan several times before the children disappeared, which led us to realize that those two were in on it together. The plan was to make it look like Tina had murdered the children and then killed herself on top of it. That way, Bryan would have a clean slate and could start over. Bette admitted to it all and also said that the plan was for her to take her husband, Darryl, hiking and then push him over a cliff. She said it was Bryan's plan and that once she got there with her husband, she couldn't do it. She's blaming it all on Bryan, but I'm not buying it. She's been of great help, though. With her testimony along with Becky's and her mother's and all the phone records, his many calls to Hutcheon, and the money he transferred, I think we're building a pretty good case against him."

"How's Hutcheon doing?"

"I haven't seen him myself, but I have been checking up on him. They say he will be fine. Some physical therapy to make sure his arm works properly is needed, but other than that, he's okay."

"The world probably won't mourn the loss of another great paparazzi photographer if he doesn't get it to work, though."

That made me laugh. "He will be charged with the attempted kidnapping of Elena Gasgarth, so we'll see what happens with that."

"Lizards, reptiles, and monsters, huh?" Dana said. "Oh, my. I guess they do live among us."

She winked, and we walked inside Becky's room. Her mother was sitting by her side, holding her hand. Becky's face lit up, and I strapped the balloons to the end of her bed.

THE END

Afterword

Dear Reader,

Thank you for purchasing *Say It Isn't So (Eva Rae Thomas #12)*. What a crazy ride this book was—for me to write, at least. I hope you enjoyed it just as much. Now, as usual, I haven't made all of this up. There was actually a dad who was arrested for murdering his children because he believed they were half reptiles and would grow into becoming lizard monsters. Yes, it is true, and it gave me inspiration for parts of this book. You can read more here:

https://www.cbs8.com/article/news/local/father-charged-with-murdering-kids-may-have-believed-lizard-people/509-309c60f3-02d3-49f0-931f-56bcd2d37e46

Also, the fact that conspiracy theories can be hard on marriages and relationships was something I read about in an article. In it, some people talked about how it destroyed their lives. You can read more here:

https://www.salon.com/2021/02/27/meet-the-spouses-whose-marriages-were-destroyed-by-qanon/

And there was actually a little girl who survived her father's rage when he tried to kill her and her sister by pretending she was dead. I was very impressed with her and wanted to use it for my book. You can read about her here:

https://www.wesh.com/article/florida-child-plays-dead-dad-stabbing/40690754

As always, I want to thank you for all your support and remind you to leave a review of this book if you can. It means the world to me.

Take care,

Willow

About the Author

Willow Rose is a multi-million-copy best-selling Author and an Amazon ALL-star Author of more than 80 novels.

Several of her books have reached the top 10 of ALL books on Amazon in the US, UK, and Canada. She has sold more than three million books all over the world.

She writes Mystery, Thriller, Paranormal, Romance, Suspense, Horror, Supernatural thrillers, and Fantasy.

Willow's books are fast-paced, nail-biting, page-turners with twists you won't see coming. That's why her fans call her The Queen of Scream.

Willow lives on Florida's Space Coast with her husband and two daughters. When she is not writing or reading, you will find her surfing and watch the dolphins play in the waves of the Atlantic Ocean.

Join Willow Rose's VIP Newsletter to get exclusive updates about New Releases, Giveaways, and FREE ebooks.
Just scan this QR code with your phone and click on the link:

SCAN ME

Win a waterproof Kindle e-reader or a $125 Amazon giftcard!
Just become a member of my Facebook group **WILLOW ROSE - MYSTERY SERIES**.
Every time we pass 1000 new members, we'll randomly select a winner from all the entries.

To enter go here:
https://www.facebook.com/groups/1921072668197253

Tired of too many emails? Text the word: "willowrose" to 31996 to sign up to Willow's VIP text List to get a text alert with news about New Releases, Giveaways, Bargains and Free books from Willow.

Follow Willow Rose on BookBub here: https://www.book-bub.com/authors/willow-rose

Follow Willow on BookBub

Connect with Willow online:
https://www.facebook.com/willowredrose
https://twitter.com/madamwillowrose
http://www.goodreads.com/author/show/4804769.Willow_Rose
https://www.willow-rose.net
Mail to: contact@willow-rose.net

Ingram Content Group UK Ltd.
Milton Keynes UK
UKHW040753030723
424469UK00001B/152